CUCKOO
SUMMER

CUCKOO SUMMER

Jonathan Tulloch

ANDERSEN PRESS

First published in Great Britain in 2022 by
Andersen Press Limited
20 Vauxhall Bridge Road, London SW1V 2SA, UK
Vijverlaan 48, 3062 HL Rotterdam, Nederland
www.andersenpress.co.uk

2 4 6 8 10 9 7 5 3 1

British Library Cataloguing in Publication Data available.

ISBN 978 1 83913 209 4

Printed and bound in Great Britain by
Clays Ltd, Elcograf S.p.A.

As always for Shirley and Aidan

Westmorland Sheep Counting Numbers

Yan	1
Tan	2
Tethera	3
Methera	4
Pimp	5
Sethera	6
Lethera	7
Hovera	8
Dovera	9
Dick	10
Yan-a-dick	11
Tan-a-dick	12
Tethera-a-dick	13
Methera-a-dick	14
Bumfit	15
Yan-a-bumfit	16
Tan-a-bumfit	17
Tethera-a-bumfit	18
Methera-a-bumfit	19
Giggot	20

June 1940. Woundale,
the Lake District,
England

YAN ...

1

It was Sally who found him. She came sprinting back down through the trees to tell me. 'Tommy! Tommy!' she cried. 'You'll never guess what.'

'What?'

'He's in the old oak,' she said breathlessly.

'Who is?'

'Just hanging there. Legs dangling doon.' Sally was an evacuee from Tyneside. She didn't speak like us. Especially when she was excited: 'Tommy man, his parachute's all tangled up in the branches.'

'Parachute?'

'That's what I'm telling you. It's a German airman. He must have jumped oot when that plane went over last night.'

Last night a German plane had flown low over Woundale. The first one we'd heard since the war began. By the roaring din, I'd guessed it was a Heinkel bomber.

I started running towards the tarn.

'Where you going, Tommy?' Sally cried.

'To tell someone,' I said. 'We've got to report him.'

'Divvent,' she called.

I'd known Sally long enough to understand most of her words by now. Divvent meant — don't. Even if I hadn't understood, the tone of her voice would have made me stop.

'Divvent report him,' she repeated. 'Not yet. Come and see him first.'

'But he's an enemy combatant,' I said. 'We have to inform the authorities.'

'Well, that's where you're wrong,' she replied.

'What do you mean?'

'He's neeone's enemy, Tommy. You see, he's dead.'

'How do you know?' I asked.

'I've seen dead ones and I've seen live ones,' Sally said. 'And that German gadgie's not climbing doon from that tree any time soon.'

Gadgie — a man.

'Want to come and see him, Tommy?' Sally asked.

I didn't, but Sally was never frightened of anything, so I followed her up into the woods that grew on the steep side of the dale. Sally was the sort of person you would follow — even when you didn't want to.

'Told you he was dead, didn't I?' she said when we reached the tree. 'Look at his heed hanging like a pit pony's after a double shift. Howay, Tom, come nearer; you cannet see him properly from back there.'

4

'I'm all right here,' I said, but I shuffled forward.

'Think he snuffed it when he hit the tree?' she whispered. 'Or was he already dead?'

I tried to speak, but my mouth was too dry. I'd never seen a dead person before. I looked up into the tree. All knobbly and gnarled, it was the oldest oak in Woundale. The first thing I saw was the dead man's boots. They were long and black, and reached up to his knees. I couldn't bring myself to look at the rest of him. From somewhere deeper in the wood, the cuckoo began to call.

'We'll still have to report it,' I managed to say. 'We'll have to—'

But Sally wasn't listening. She'd picked up a long branch and was walking towards the dangling airman.

'What you doing, Sal?' I gasped.

'Got to make sure,' she said. 'Got to see for certain he is a goner.'

I began to back away.

'Just a little poke,' I heard her murmur, as she lifted the branch into the tree.

I turned and started to run back down through the woods. I hadn't gone far when I heard Sally shriek. A moment later, she came crashing after me through the trees.

'He's not dead!' she shouted.

2

Hurtling down the steep dale side, we burst out of the woods and sprinted round the tarn to where I lived with my three aunties. My hobnailed boots kicked dust up from the path. Sally's thick, black hair flew out behind her like a galloping horse's tail as she overtook me. She turned and laughed, showing the gap between her two front teeth — the kind of gap that Sally said meant you were born lucky. She shot through the farmyard and was waiting at the door of our whitewashed stone farmhouse when I arrived.

Before I could get in the house though, the door was flung open in our faces, and Mr Scarcross came rushing out. He was carrying his shotgun. 'There's a Nazi on the loose,' he growled.

Auntie Gladys and Auntie Dolly dashed out of the farmhouse behind him. They were wearing their pinnies. It was baking day.

'That German bomber we heard fly over last night,' Auntie Dolly blurted, the thick curls of her ginger hair flecked with flour. 'It crash-landed in town.'

'Came down right in the middle of the churchyard,' Auntie Gladys explained breathlessly, her eyes a brilliant blue behind her round, wire-framed glasses. She was carrying Vi, my two-year-old cousin.

'Postman says there's supposed to be five in the crew,' Auntie Dolly went on.

'But they only found four bodies,' Auntie Gladys added. 'They're saying one of them must have parachuted out.'

'We've only just heard,' said Auntie Dolly, pointing to where the postman could be seen, pushing his bike up the steep road which climbs out of Woundale onto the fells.

I tried to speak, to tell them about the German airman, but they were talking so quickly I couldn't get a word in edgeways. Besides, you weren't allowed to interrupt grown-ups.

'Four of them in their seats,' said Scarcross. 'Burnt to—'

'Not in front of the children, Mr Scarcross,' said Auntie Annie, coming out behind the others.

Mr Scarcross grinned sourly. 'You know what they say, Miss Grisedale. The only good Jerry is a dead Jerry.'

None of us liked Mr Scarcross, but Auntie Annie said we had to get on with him. He was our only neighbour — there were just two farmhouses in Woundale, ours and his, with a few fields and the tarn between. Sally was Mr Scarcross's evacuee. Tall and very thin, his thick grey hair was always slicked back with barber's grease. Sally said it was pig's lard. One of his eyes was made out of glass. He'd lost the real one in the last war. But you could never tell which was which, because neither eye ever blinked. When he looked at you, it felt like being stared at by a snake.

'They don't know where the missing one is,' Auntie Dolly said. 'But they think he was the navigator.'

'Postman said he might have landed here in Woundale,' continued Auntie Gladys.

'Postman said he might have parachuted into the tarn,' shivered Auntie Dolly.

'Or somewhere in the woods,' added Auntie Gladys.

'Stuff and nonsense,' said Auntie Annie, adjusting the topknot of her brown headscarf that she wore all day, every day, except Sundays. 'He could have come down anywhere for miles around.'

'Well,' snarled Mr Scarcross, tapping his shotgun grimly. 'If he is in Woundale, I'll catch him. Then he'll wish he'd gone down with the others.' He glared at Sally and me. 'What about you two? Not seen anything of him, have you?'

No sooner had I said 'Yes', Sally burst out 'No.'

I looked at her in confusion.

'Well, which is it?' Mr Scarcross demanded. 'Did you see the Jerry or not?'

'Thought we saw someone, didn't we?' said Sally quickly, before I could speak again. 'But it wasn't neeone. Just a deer. Wasn't it, Tommy man? Just a deer hiding in the trees.'

I felt her foot nudging mine. 'Just a deer,' I heard myself say.

'Chuffing hell,' spat Mr Scarcross. 'Bit of a difference between a Nazi and a flippin' deer.'

'We were playing,' Sally explained. 'We weren't looking for nee Nazis.'

'Where were you playing?' Auntie Annie asked, looking closely at me. She had the same blue eyes as my other aunties, but she always seemed to see more.

'By the tarn,' Sally said, just as I was saying, 'In the woods.'

'Ee, God,' said Mr Scarcross. 'Yon lass is such a liar; she'd fib to the devil himself.'

'We were playing in the woods first,' said Sally. 'Then we went by the tarn.'

'Well, I can't stand here blethering all day,' said Mr Scarcross. 'We've a Hun on the run.' He pointed his gun straight at Sally. 'Now, Missy Liar. Never mind playing, you get yourself back and feed my hens. Think I keep an evacuee so she can go larking about whenever she's a mind to?'

'But it's Saturday afternoon,' said Sally.

'Don't backchat me,' Mr Scarcross snapped. 'And once you've fed the hens, you can muck out the byre an' all. Or there'll be no tea for you.' Mr Scarcross's snake eyes turned to my aunties. 'I don't know why you let your Tommy play with that one. She's wilder than a weasel. You wouldn't believe what she gets up to. Any road, I'd best search the dale. Maybe you ladies should lock your doors tonight, just until Fritz the airman's been caught, wherever he is.'

And with that Mr Scarcross strode away along the tarn,

where Silent Simon was waiting. Silent Simon was Mr Scarcross's farm worker.

Sally headed off too. Taking the path round the other side of the tarn towards the Scarcross farm, she was doing that walk of hers that tells the whole world she doesn't care. Head up like a cockerel crowing on a byre roof, arms swinging and feet kicking high — as though she had just scored a penalty for Newcastle United in a cup final. Only I knew that when she walked like this, she felt more like someone who'd just missed one. I hated the fact that she was Mr Scarcross's evacuee, and so did Sally. He made her work all the time, and often kept her short of food. But there was nothing we could do about it. As everyone kept saying, there was a war on — the Germans might invade at any time.

The cuckoo was still calling. Its two-note song echoed from the woods where the airman was hanging by his parachute.

3

'Are you going to tell me what all that was about?' Auntie Annie asked me when Sally had gone.

'We saw a deer,' I replied.

'Tom-Tom deer!' babbled my young cousin Vi, wriggling to be free from Auntie Gladys's arm. Now that Mr Scarcross had gone, she was wasn't frightened any more. I forced myself to smile.

'Not got anything else to say, Tommy?' Auntie Annie said.

Staring at the bow of her headscarf topknot which stuck up like a pair of rabbit ears, I shook my head. Why had Sally wanted to keep the airman a secret? It felt wrong not to tell the truth. I'd never lied to my aunties before. Just as well Mr Scarcross would soon find the airman for himself, and no one would ever know that we'd seen him first.

'Come on then, young Tommy,' said Auntie Annie. 'Our hens need feeding as well.'

'What about the Nazi airman?' Auntie Dolly asked.

'What about him?' Auntie Annic replied.

'Is it safe to be outside?'

'Shouldn't we lock ourselves in until Mr Scarcross catches him?' put in Auntie Gladys.

'Oh, he could be anywhere in Westmorland, Cumberland or Lancashire,' said Auntie Annie. 'Come here a minute, Thomas. You've snagged your woolly.'

I looked at the arm of my pullover. I must have caught it in the trees when I was running from the airman.

'Give it to me tonight,' Auntie Annie said. 'I'll darn it. And I think it's about time I cut your hair as well.' Auntie Annie ruffled my ginger hair. 'Just like our Dolly's,' she said, then added quietly, 'and your dad's too.'

All three of my aunties looked at me sadly. They often looked at me like that — ever since we'd heard my dad was missing in action. His plane had gone down a few weeks ago over Dunkirk.

But there isn't much time to mope on a wartime farm. Auntie Annie thrust the hen feed bucket at me. 'And once you've fed the hens, don't forget to water Mavis,' she said. Mavis was our pig. 'And the tattie patch needs weeding, I've done a good half of it to start you off.'

We worked hard on our farm. Every day was the same. Rise with the sun and do your jobs. Go to school. Come home from school, and do more jobs. Sometimes miss school, to do even more jobs. Go to bed at sunset. Then begin it all again the next day. When Sally had arrived with the evacuation though, life had changed. She'd brought excitement and fun — lots of fun. It had been like spring arriving after a long winter. We still had to work, but with Sally around there would always be adventures. You just never knew what was going to happen next. And since my dad had been missing in action, Sally was the only one who could make me laugh when I felt sad.

As my aunties and Vi disappeared back into the house, a delicious smell of baking bread wafted out. Not even the arrival of Hitler himself would keep my aunties from the kitchen on baking day.

'Chuck, chuck,' I called, clanking the metal feed bucket.

The hens came clucking over. Usually, you have to feed them carefully so that there's nothing left for the rats. But today as I scattered the potato skins and sprouted corn, I kept one eye on the woods — how long would it take Mr Scarcross to find the airman? Not long. The old oak grew above the footpath through the woods. Would he march him away, or was the airman injured? How would Mr Scarcross get him out of the tree? Would he send me to town to fetch the Home Guard while he guarded the oak?

A small flock of sparrows burst from the eaves of the house and joined the hens pecking for food at my feet. Still watching the woods, I took the empty bucket down to the tarn, close to where the bulrushes grew. It was easier than filling it at the pump. Back in the byre I poured the water into Mavis's trough. Mavis was a saddleback sow. She grunted happily. Lying in the shadows, she was suckling her piglets. It took four buckets to fill Mavis's water trough and I was going back to the tarn for the second bucket when I heard the cuckoo call again. This time it was much closer. It had flown into the reeds. Only it wasn't the cuckoo — it was Sally.

Sally could imitate all sorts of sounds by whistling through the lucky gap in her teeth: trill like a thrush, hoot like an owl, call like a cuckoo. And I was the only one who could tell it was her. Sally was calling me.

Dropping the bucket, I pushed my way deep into the bulrushes where we'd cleared a space and made one of our dens.

'You took your time, bonny lad,' she said.

'Why did you tell them we hadn't seen him?' I shot back.

'Had to,' she replied. 'Anyway, howay, we haven't got a moment to lose.'

'What do you mean?'

'We've got to gan back to him.'

'Go back to who?'

'The airman.'

I couldn't believe my ears. 'What are you talking about? Mr Scarcross is looking for him.'

'That's what I'm worried aboot, man,' Sally said. 'If Snakecross finds him, he'll shoot him before he has a chance to surrender.'

'No, he won't,' I returned, shocked by her words. 'There are rules for dealing with captured enemy combatants.'

'He has his own rules, Tom.'

'The airman will surrender and Mr Scarcross will have to hand him over as a prisoner of war. Mr Scarcross was in the last war. And he's in the Home Guard. He'll know what you have to do.'

Sally's voice dropped low. 'The only good Jerry is a dead Jerry — that's what he said.'

'Lots of people say that.'

'Aye, but he means it. There's nowt he's not capable of.' All at once, Sally's voice grew small. 'You wouldn't believe the cruel things I've seen him dee, Tommy. And when he came oot of your hoose with his shotgun, I knew exactly what he'd do to the airman if he caught him — same thing that he does to every poor creature he catches in a trap. Well, this time I'm going to stop him.' Her voice rose: 'Howay, we've got to get to that airman before Scarecross. Are you with me, or do you want him to gun doon a defenceless gadgie hanging in a tree?'

'But even if Mr Scarcross does want to shoot him, how can we stop him?' I demanded.

Sally's dark eyes sparked like struck matches. 'I divvent kna. Let's gan and find oot. Are you with me?'

'Yes, I'm with you.'

'Champion.'

With that she burst out of the bulrushes and started running to the woods. And I followed. I always followed Sally.

'Champion' was one of my favourite Sally words. It meant that everything was tickety-boo. But I didn't feel that everything was champion. Perhaps even then I sensed that this was the beginning of an adventure unlike any we'd had before — or would ever know again.

4

We slipped into the woods. 'Keep your eyes peeled for Smellycross,' Sally murmured. 'Or he'll end up shooting us instead. You divvent kna him like I dee, Tom.'

We walked on in silence for a while. 'Are you sure the German airman was still alive?' I whispered.

She nodded.

'How could you tell?' I pressed. 'Did he say something to you?'

'Mebbees.'

'Maybe? What did he say?'

'He said, "Oi, divvent poke us with that long thin stick!" How do I know what he said, Thomas man? Divvent speak Jerry, do I? Howay, we'd better creep up on him from behind. Just in case he's got a knife, or a machine gun.'

'German navigators won't be armed with machine guns,' I pointed out. 'But all flight personnel are issued with Luftwaffe Lugers.'

'What's one of them when it's at home, Tommy?'

'A pistol.'

Leaving the path, we worked our way up through the steep woods until we were in the trees just above the old oak.

'You frightened, Tommy?' breathed Sally.

I nodded. 'Are you?'

'Why aye, bonny lad,' replied Sally, but her eyes were still blazing with excitement.

We crept down to the old oak. Sally went first. Turning round, she put her tongue out to encourage me, and as I forced myself to do the same, there was an explosion in the trees above. The blood was still rushing in my ears when I realised it was just a woodpigeon.

Since I was wearing shorts, I had to stop myself from shouting out as we waded through a patch of stinging nettles. Like my aunties, Sally wore 'land girl kecks'. Handknit for female farm workers, they were thick woollen trousers with deep pockets.

At last, we'd reached the old oak. All we had to do was creep round the trunk, and the German airman would be above us, his long black boots dangling down. Suddenly I felt sick. I'd lied to Sally. I wasn't just frightened. I was petrified.

'I can hear him breathing,' she whispered. 'Can you?'

All I could hear was the wind murmuring through the trees.

'Quiet as spiders, now, Tommy. Divvent cough, or snap a twig. Divvent pump . . .'

But Sally didn't move, and neither did I. I listened with every fibre of my being, but I still couldn't hear the German airman breathing. I couldn't hear anything, except the restless wind, the cuckoo calling and the thumping of my own heart.

Then, to my horror, Sally suddenly called out: 'We're not going to hurt you, Jerry gadgie.' And walking calmly round to the other side of the tree, she looked up. 'Tommy man,' she said. 'Come and look.'

I forced myself to follow. When I looked up into the old oak, I saw only the gnarled branches of the ancient tree.

'He's gone,' said Sally.

5

There was no sign of the German airman; there was no sign of his parachute.

'Vanished,' Sally said.

'How did he get down?'

'How do I know?' she replied. 'Mebbees he chewed his way oot. Or grew wings and flew away.'

'Where's he gone?'

'Your guess is as good as mine, Tommy man.'

'Mr Scarcross must have found him already,' I said.

As though to check the airman wasn't hiding somewhere in the tree above, Sally snatched a stick and hurled it up. The stick clattered loudly into the branches and lodged there. We were both staring up, when a shot rang out.

We crashed back through the nettles and hurled ourselves into a thicket of purple foxgloves. Just in time. Mr Scarcross was striding through the trees, his shotgun still smoking.

He looked up at the tree. He must have heard Sally throw the stick.

'Flamin' pigeons,' he said. 'Thought it was the Jerry.'

Sally glanced at me. 'Hasn't found him yet,' she mouthed.

She'd been right. Mr Scarcross wasn't interested in giving the enemy airman a chance to surrender. He would shoot him as soon as he saw him.

'Hey, Numpty, get yourself here,' Mr Scarcross called over his shoulder.

Peering out carefully from our hiding place, we saw Silent Simon lumbering over to Mr Scarcross. Though big, Silent Simon was gentle. If Mr Scarcross was like a snake, Silent Simon was a huge but friendly bull. His brown hair was cropped close.

'Let's just double check there's no Nazi hiding round here,' Mr Scarcross said. 'Have a good look.'

Gun at the ready, Mr Scarcross prowled around the oak. Silent Simon began searching the undergrowth.

'Look properly, you great dunderhead,' said Mr Scarcross. 'Or I'll give you what for.'

We watched Silent Simon working his way towards us. The foxgloves were in full bloom, and a white-tailed bumblebee buzzed loudly inside one of the flowers. Silent Simon came closer and closer, his huge hands parting the grass and flowers. Then there he was, staring right at us.

'Seen something?' Mr Scarcross demanded.

Silent Simon opened his mouth as though to reply. At that moment, Sally shook her head and put a finger to her lips.

'Well?' Mr Scarcross demanded.

Silent Simon straightened up. Shaking his head, he stood so that Mr Scarcross couldn't see us.

Mr Scarcross swore. 'Come on then, we'll search up by the force.'

The force was what we call the waterfall at the head of the valley, behind our farmhouse. Mr Scarcross hurried away, followed by Silent Simon.

'Come on, Sally,' I said. 'I've had enough of this. Let's go and tell Auntie Annie.'

'Whisht, haad your gob,' she replied.

Whisht, haad your gob — be quiet, shut your mouth. Closing her eyes, Sally began whispering to herself.

'What you doing, Sal?'

'What's it look like? Counting to a hundred, aren't I? To make sure Scarecrow's really gone.'

I sat back down amongst the foxgloves. Once she'd counted to a hundred, she started counting from a hundred backwards.

'Come on, Sally, don't be silly.'

'You have to!' she exclaimed. 'For someone as nasty as Stinkcross you've got to make double sure he's gone.'

When she'd finished, we ran down through the woods. But at the tarn, she carried on for the Scarcross place.

'Where are you going?' I called.

'Got jobs to do, haven't I?'

'I thought we were telling Auntie Annie about the German airman.'

'Tell her what?' Sally demanded. 'That when we found him, we didn't let on. And it's only now that we've lost him that we're telling her? Then we really would be in trouble — proper police trouble. And what do you think Scarcross would do to me if he found out I'd lied about a German? Besides, there's nee need to blab. You see, he's gone. He won't even be in Woundale any more. He'll be miles away by now. You divvent hang around when you're playing the wag.'

'The wag?'

She nodded. 'When you're flitting, scarpering, doing a bunk, running away. And the first rule of playing the wag? Gan as far as you can, as quick as you can.'

'How do you know?'

'Cos I know everything.'

'No, I mean, how do you know about playing the wag? Have you run away before, Sal?'

'Did you see Snailcross's face when he was looking up into that tree?' Sally laughed, and then imitated Mr Scarcross's fixed stare.

Sally always did this. Whenever I tried to ask her about her life before she came to live in Woundale, she would never answer. Instead, she'd tell a joke, or pretend to be Scarcross when he was drunk or swatting a fly. All I knew about her was that she was from Tyneside. She never wrote any letters home, like the other evacuees at school. Never got any either. Never mentioned her mam and dad.

'Anyhow, you heard Smellycross,' she said. 'If I divvent dee them jobs, I'll have nee tea.'

And with that, she continued along the tarn.

I followed.

'Haven't you got any jobs of your own, Tommy man?' she called over her shoulder.

'I'm going to help you finish yours,' I said.

'Divvent need nee help, me,' she returned. 'Never have. Never will.'

Despite this, I could tell that she didn't mind me coming. I smiled. 'Thought a townie like you might need someone who knows what they're doing,' I said.

'Mind you divvent trip up in them big boots of yours,' she replied.

6

The Scarcross place was not like our farm. His animals were badly fed. His outbuildings were dilapidated. An abandoned plough rusted in his yard. A large barrel stood by the water pump. If Mr Scarcross's farmhouse had ever been whitewashed, it must have been a long time ago, because now it was grey as Lakeland slate. It looked like a huge boulder that a giant had pushed down from the fellside above and no one had been able to roll back up.

No sparrows lived in the eaves of the Scarcross farmhouse. If they did, he shot them. But not even Mr Scarcross could stop the daisies growing. Thick drifts of them were poking up, hiding the spent shotgun cartridges that littered the farmyard.

As Sally fed Mr Scarcross's hens, the poor half-starved creatures pecked viciously at each other. 'I think they might need more feed,' I said.

'Nowt left in the meal bin, man,' Sally snapped.

'I'll show you what we do when our hens are still hungry,' I said.

'If I wanted a lesson, I'd gan to school,' Sally returned.

But all the same, she followed me down to the tarn. And when I started picking up the water snails from the shallows and popping them into her bucket, she did the same. One of the things I'd learnt about Sally was that she was like a hedgehog — even if she liked you, she couldn't help her prickles. But once she trusted you, she unrolled.

'Do they like snails?' she asked.

'As much as we like fish and chips,' I said.

Before the war, Dad took us on the train to the seaside every summer, and we always had fish and chips.

'Divvent gan on aboot fish and chips,' said Sally. 'It's making me mouth water. That's the only thing I miss from back there.'

She always called Tyneside 'back there'. Never said it was home.

'Back there,' she carried on, 'you can smell fish and chips on every street corner.'

'Don't you miss anything else — from back there?' I asked.

With a grin, she threw a clump of waterweed at me. 'Funny how life turns oot,' she said. 'I might have been born a princess, but here I am picking up snails with a farm boy. A farm boy who needs a haircut.'

I threw the weed back. It lodged in her hair.

'Seen me feather boa?' she demanded, flourishing the long, thick frond of waterweed. 'Me name's Duchess La-di-da.'

Laughing, she pranced up and down the shore, kicking water at me.

I kicked water back. Nearly helpless with laughter, we kicked water and hurled handfuls of weed at each other. That was what Sally was like. No matter where she was or what was happening, she was never far from laughter.

Still chuckling, I stared over the tarn. From here I could see my whole world. The bulrushes hiding one of our dens, the woods, and our whitewashed farmhouse standing across the water at the head of the dale. Members of my family had been tenant farmers in Woundale since my great-grandfather's time. Just like the Scarcrosses. Behind our house, you could just see the force, its foaming water flashing white. And over everything — the shimmering call of the cuckoo. It had flown into the bulrushes.

'Does he really come from far away?' Sally suddenly asked.

'Who?'

'The cuckoo. You told me he comes from the other side of the world.'

I nodded. 'Africa. He only stays here for a while, then he goes back.'

'Did your dad tell you that?'

'Yes.'

'He tells you lots of things, doesn't he, Tommy?'

I nodded again.

Sally smiled. 'He'll be all right, you know,' she said gently.

'Your dad. They'll find him. He'll have parachuted oot of his plane, just like the Jerry. He'll come home.'

My aunties always said that to me as well. The difference was that Sally really believed it. And more than that; when she said it — I believed it too. Maybe that's why I always followed her when she asked me to.

'Do you know something else he told me about the cuckoo, Sally?'

'What?'

'Cuckoos never know their real mams and dads.'

Her eyes widened. 'Why not?'

'You see, the cuckoo lays her eggs in another bird's nest. And that bird brings the babies up. The babies never see their parents.'

'So that's why he sings all the time,' Sally whispered.

Now it was my turn to ask: 'What do you mean?'

'So, the babies know their dad's nearby.'

For a while we both gathered snails from the tarn, listening to the cuckoo. When we'd collected enough, Sally took the bucket back to the farmyard.

'Why didn't Silent Simon let on he'd seen us?' I called after her.

'Divvent worry aboot him, man,' Sally said. 'He won't blab. He's me marra.'

Marra — mate.

Smelling the snails, the hens came cackling round Sally.

She emptied the bucket in a pile, and the hens began fighting and pecking at each other. The cockerel too.

Quickly, I snatched up handfuls of the snails and scattered them. 'So the hens don't fight too much,' I explained.

'Funny old world, isn't it?' Sally said. 'Sometimes it seems we're all at war. Even the hens.'

As Sally collected the eggs, I started mucking out the Scarcross byre. It had to be done before he came back, otherwise he really wouldn't give her any tea. It was a gloomy place. One of the main wooden beams hung down like a broken leg. I hadn't been working long when I heard a sigh from the shadows. It was Mr Scarcross's Clydesdale. Chestnut and white, this massive horse was a gentle giant. I tried to call him from the shadows, but though his head was almost high enough to reach the rafters, he was nervous — Scarcross always mistreated him.

The only things that didn't feel downtrodden in that byre were the swallows. They had a nest in the rafters, and kept flying in to feed their young.

I was watching a swallow swoop up to its nest when the horse suddenly snorted and came at me. I barred his way with the graip — the fork we use to muck out with. But he didn't want to hurt me. Sally was standing in the doorway, and he just wanted to say hello to her.

'Hello, Arnold,' she said, and went over to bury her face in the heavy horse's thick, black mane.

Scarcross had never given any of his animals a name, but Sally called him Arnold.

'Now then, marra,' she said to the horse. 'Got something for you.'

And she brought out a carrot.

'Where did you get that from?' I asked.

'Never you mind,' Sally shot back, then taking a bite from the carrot herself, she held the rest of it out to Arnold.

The horse pulled back its great lips and chomped on the carrot.

'You've got a way with animals,' I said. 'Usually, folk have to be born to it.'

'Have I, Tommy?'

I nodded. 'We'll make a country lass of you yet.'

Patting Arnold, she grabbed my graip. 'Now, I'll show you how it's done.' And she began forking the dirty straw into the barrow.

I got another graip, and we worked quickly together. Ducking whenever the swallows darted in to feed their chicks in the nest, we forked and carted five barrowloads of soiled straw out to the midden. Then laid the fresh straw.

'Cheers, marra,' Sally said when we'd finished. 'Now, get yourself home. Them aunties of yours will be wondering where their bonny lad's rambled off to. Specially if they think that airman's aboot. But divvent worry, he'll probably have been taken prisoner by now. Not by Stinksnake but a proper soldier who won't shoot him if he's got his hands in the air.'

7

After we'd had our tea and finished our evening jobs, Auntie Annie did something she'd never done before. As the old clock struck nine, she locked the house door.

'If there is a German airman, he'll have been apprehended by now,' she said, 'but if this keeps the pair of you quiet.' And she turned the key and pulled the bolt.

'But if the Jerry is in Woundale, do you think a locked door will be enough to keep him out?' Auntie Dolly asked.

'Won't he just kick his way in?' Auntie Gladys said.

'Or shoot the bolt off with his gun?' Auntie Dolly wondered.

'And what about the windows?' put in Auntie Gladys. 'He could easily climb in through them.' And she wiped her glasses clean, as though to be able to spot the German airman more clearly.

'If he really did land in Woundale,' Auntie Annie responded, 'Mr Scarcross would have found him or his parachute by now. He's looked everywhere. Now come on, Tommy, it's way past your bedtime.'

Something else happened for the first time. Auntie Annie

was letting Connie, my border collie, sleep upstairs with me. As a working dog, Connie always slept in a kennel outside.

Old farmhouses can't keep secrets. There was a disused fireplace downstairs, and if you sat on the wide windowsill in my room, the voices of anyone talking in the kitchen came right up to you, clear as a wireless. I don't think anyone else knew about it; just me and my dad. He told me he used to sit on the same windowsill and listen to the grown-ups when he was a lad. And tonight, after I'd gone upstairs to bed, instead of sleeping I sat there with Connie listening to every word my aunties said.

'I won't sleep a wink tonight,' Auntie Dolly was saying, her voice shuddering. 'The postman said that somewhere up Carlisle way, a German spy threw a hand grenade into a house.'

'Popped it right through the letterbox,' added Auntie Gladys. 'When everyone was in bed.'

'Just as well we haven't got a letterbox then,' Auntie Annie replied.

The postman always delivered his letters straight onto our kitchen table, where he was given a cup of tea. As well as bringing any letters, the postman also brought the gossip from town and further afield. Town had a church and a chapel, a few shops and our school. I thought it was big but Sally said it was nothing more than a street. Further afield was the rest of the world. That huge, strange place beyond our land of mountains and lakes. The place where the cuckoo had come from. The place where Sally had come from too.

'Postman said,' Auntie Dolly continued, 'that in Scotland ...'

'A Nazi spy hid under someone's bed,' Auntie Gladys put in.

'For two days,' said Auntie Dolly.

'Postman said,' said Auntie Gladys, 'that a Jerry locked himself in someone's outdoor privy ...'

'And they only found him when they tried to use it,' said Auntie Dolly.

'Postman said a Jerry hid in someone's byre,' said Auntie Gladys.

'And was signalling to a U-boat submarine just off the coast,' Auntie Dolly said.

'Postman said that this could be the start of the invasion,' Auntie Gladys said. 'He said, just look how quickly Belgium has fallen, and France is sure to surrender in a couple of days too.'

'Postman said,' chorused Auntie Gladys and Auntie Dolly together, 'we're next.'

'Is there anything that postman doesn't say?' Auntie Annie's voice rose. 'He could talk the hind legs off a donkey. What he doesn't know, he makes up.'

For a long time, nothing else was said. The wireless wasn't even on — Auntie Gladys and Dolly wanted to be able to hear if the German airman tried to climb in through the windows. The silence felt deep as the tarn. The only sound was the tick of the grandfather clock and the furious click of needles. My aunties were always knitting. I could picture them as clearly as though I was sitting with them. Auntie Dolly with her ginger hair rolled into curls. She wrapped her hair round old rags every night — to make her curls. Auntie Gladys's piercing blue eyes shining through her glasses as she concentrated hard on the needles. Still wearing her brown headscarf, Auntie Annie knitting at twice the speed of the other two. They were knitting for Uncle John, Auntie Gladys's husband; he was a soldier who had managed to come back safely from Dunkirk. Knitting for little Vi — Auntie Gladys and Uncle John's daughter. Knitting for Auntie Dolly's boyfriend, Stan Hawkrigg, a member of the Home Guard. Knitting a pullover for me and a cardigan for Sally. Every night their needles clacked away like ack-ack guns aimed on enemy aircraft; firing scarves, hats, gloves, pullovers and long john combinations. It was their way of fighting the war. And everything knitted with wool sheared and then spun from our own sheep. They didn't realise that I knew that there was one person in the family who they weren't knitting for any more — my dad. They might say to me that he was coming back, but deep down I think they feared the worst.

'We should have Connie back out on the yard,' Auntie Gladys suddenly burst out. 'She'd sharp start barking if the invasion begins.'

'Speak sense,' Auntie Annie snapped. 'There is no invasion.

Not tonight anyway. I've let the dog upstairs for our Tommy. Didn't you notice he was a bit quiet earlier? Has been for a good while. Ever since his dad went missing. I'm worried about him. He never says much about his dad. But I can tell he thinks about him all the time.'

'If only our Arthur hadn't joined the RAF,' said Auntie Dolly.

Our Arthur — my dad.

'I told him not to,' said Auntie Gladys. 'I told my John not to join up as well. Farming is a reserved occupation. The country needs to feed itself before it can fight. But they wouldn't listen.'

'There's a war on,' said Auntie Annie. 'You do what needs doing. Only I hope to God he does come back. With Tommy already losing his mam.'

Though they were whispering now, I could still hear every word.

'He's been missing a month,' Auntie Dolly said.

'You'd have thought we would have heard by now,' said Auntie Gladys.

'Aye,' said Auntie Annie. 'We'll continue praying for the best, but we have to prepare for the worst.'

Getting off the windowsill, I went over to where a framed photo stood on the dresser. It was the only photo I had. I picked it up. On the black and white picture, my mam and dad were standing smiling by the tarn, and I was with them, a baby cuddled in my mam's arms. She died not long after this was taken. Sometimes I would close my eyes very tightly to try and catch a glimpse of her face, or a fleeting memory. But I only ever saw her in my dreams. My dad was all that I had left of her. He often told me things that she'd said or done. How excited she had been to hold me in her arms on the day of the photograph. How she was always carrying me around like that and showing me her favourite flowers and birds. How much she had loved me. My dad used to say that although she had died, her love for me never would, because he wouldn't let it. That is why my dad had to come back. If I lost him, I would lose her as well.

Back on the windowsill again, I buried my face in Connie's lovely soft fur. The window was wide open so we could both gaze at the sunset. The cuckoo was calling from the reeds. The wind was playing in the trees.

'Well, I'm not going outside to use the privy,' Auntie Gladys was saying. 'Those Germans are savages. No respect for women and children. I'll stay inside with my legs crossed all night if needs be.'

'Postman said they'll likely be sending the Home Guard to search Woundale soon,' Auntie Dolly added. 'He said they were checking some of the other dales first.'

'Well, we've nothing to worry about then,' said Auntie Annie. 'I wonder if your young man will be with them, Dolly?'

Even sitting a floor above, I could imagine Auntie Dolly blush. They often gently teased her about her boyfriend Stan Hawkrigg in the Home Guard, and when she was embarrassed she would blush bright red, so her cheeks really were like a doll's. It was for Stan that Auntie Dolly made her curls. She said he liked them. To me, they just looked like two fat sausages sizzling on top of her head.

'I wondered why you were knitting that scarf so quickly,' said Auntie Gladys.

'And putting all those nice tassels on,' said Auntie Annie. 'Are you going to give it to him when he gets here?'

When all three of my Aunties suddenly laughed, it was just like an ordinary night again. Feeling cheered by the homely sound, I carefully hooked up the thick, blackout curtains, then got into bed. Connie lay down beside me.

But this was to be no ordinary night. My aunties were still joking and laughing downstairs, when I heard an owl hooting just outside my window. Suddenly the hooting became a knock. Connie let out a yelp. Then jumped off the bed. Someone was at my window.

8

I soon found out why Connie hadn't barked — she never barked at friends. It was Sally. 'Tommy man,' she whispered. 'Wake up.'

I wriggled my way through the blackout curtains. There she was clinging to the drainpipe and grinning at me through the open window.

'Areet, bonny lad?' she beamed.

'What are you doing?' I mouthed, in utter disbelief.

'Climbing me favourite beanstalk, and paying a visit to a dopey giant. What do you think I'm deein', you daft ha'p'orth — come to get you, haven't I? Did you really think I was an owl?'

'Is everything all right?' Auntie Annie called from the kitchen.

'Yes, Auntie Annie,' I called back. 'I'm just sorting out the blackout curtains.'

'Don't leave any gaps,' Auntie Dolly added.

'Hurry up,' whispered Sally. 'And come doon.'

'Down?'

'Why aye, I need your help.'

'What's wrong? Is it Mr Scarcross?'

But Sally was already shinnying back down the drainpipe. I quickly got dressed. 'Good girl,' I breathed to Connie. 'Stay.'

I climbed carefully out of the window, sat on the ledge and looked down. I was good at climbing trees, but I'd never tried a drainpipe before. Would it hold my weight? But if Sally was in trouble with Mr Scarcross then she needed my help.

'Howay,' Sally whispered up. 'It's the easiest drainpipe in the universe. Vi could climb doon it with her eyes closed. Canny loads of room for your hands. And footholds galore.'

I reached across and grabbed the pipe. It felt well secured. Hugging it, I slowly twisted round and lowered my leg, feeling for the first bracket that kept the drainpipe attached to the wall. It easily took my weight. Clinging to the drainpipe with my hands, and feeling for each foothold, I began slowly climbing down.

'Divvent take all night, marra,' Sally whispered up.

When I stepped onto the ground, Sally was already running round the tarn towards the woods. She stopped just before the trees.

'What's going on?' I demanded.

'Found him again, haven't I?' she said.

'Who?'

'The airman.'

At first, I could hardly speak. Somehow, I managed to stammer: 'In Woundale?'

'Well, he's not on the moon, marra.'

'Where?'

'I'll take you to him, Tommy. But we'll have to be careful. Cos either his gnashers are as sharp as the teeth of a Tyne dock rat, or he's got a knife. How else could he have cut himself and his parachute doon from that tree?'

'What about Mr Scarcross?'

'He's gone to town, to get the Home Guard.'

And with that she slipped into the trees. For a few moments I just stood there. In the rays of the setting sun, the woods looked as though they were on fire.

But I had to follow. How could I let her go alone?

It was much darker in the woods — the night had already arrived there. Each tree trunk seemed to hide a figure waiting to spring out. As we passed, the branches grabbed at us. When the German airman suddenly charged us, I stood there, frozen to the spot.

Only it wasn't the airman. 'Just a deer,' laughed Sally, as the shape dissolved back into the trees.

Heart thumping, I swallowed.

I could tell that though Sally was frightened, she was excited too. Silent as her own shadow, she slipped through the trees. At last, we stepped into a clearing.

'The Giant's Teeth,' I whispered.

The Giant's Teeth was a circle of nine standing stones set

in a flattish hollow. Once they must have been a lot bigger, but time had worn them down and broken them off, so that most of them were about the size of Vi. Only one of the stones, the biggest, was as tall as Sally and me. Set upright in the ground, the stones looked like a set of giant's teeth.

'Is he here?' I asked.

Sally nodded, and pointed at the dense thicket of whin bushes growing inside the stone circle. Right in the middle of the thickest part of the prickly bushes was our favourite den.

'Scarcross didn't give us nee tea tonight,' she whispered. 'So, I came to get a bit of scran from the larder.' Scran — we both used this word for food. Our larder was an old Cooperative biscuit tin we kept hidden in the den, under a pile of branches and leaves. We stored bits of scran in it for Sally: crusts of bread, heels of pie, some of last autumn's apples. 'And I couldn't believe me eyes,' Sally breathed. 'There he was fast asleep. Want to see him, Tommy man?'

Without waiting for my reply, she lifted aside our 'front door' — the branches we used to conceal the entrance to the den. Then she dropped to her hands and knees, and disappeared into the bushes. The only way to get into the den was to crawl down the low, twisting tunnel that we'd made through the thorns.

'Be careful,' I whispered, going in after her. 'Remember, he'll have a Luftwaffe Luger. And a knife.'

9

Sally had already reached the end of the tunnel and was looking into the den. 'He's still sleeping,' she whispered over her shoulder. 'His parachute's all plumped up like a pillow.'

'Is he badly hurt?'

'Got a proper nasty cut over his eye — it's curved like one of them things you cut weeds with.'

'A sickle?'

'Aye, that's the sausage.'

'Has he got a gun, or a knife?'

'Come and see for yourself.'

In the den, the bushes were so old that they'd hollowed out, and you could sit under them. It was like being in a room. We called it the 'giant's parlour'. Heart banging in my ribs like a rat in a sack, I crept forward. Then there he was, just as Sally said, sleeping like a child in the middle of the den.

It was lighter here than in the trees and the first thing I saw was his boots. Just as I remembered: black and as long as a pair of wellingtons. In the last, golden light of the long summer's day slanting in through the bushes, I could see that he was wearing the sandy-coloured, summer flight uniform of a Luftwaffe navigator — there were posters up in town of enemy uniforms, in case of an invasion. I could see too that his coveralls had two thigh pockets. Both of them were bulging. Squinting my eyes, I could just make out that there was a rip above his right knee. The shredded material was dark, with what could only be blood.

'There's Hitler's parrot,' Sally said. 'Look at it, perched on his heart.'

'That's the Nazi eagle,' I whispered, glimpsing a glimmer of the white badge of the German Luftwaffe, sewn onto the breast of the flight suit. 'Sally,' I warned. 'You're too close.'

'Have to be, divvent I?'

'Why?'

'So I can hear.'

'Hear what?'

'Whisht, I'm listening.'

'He might grab you, Sally.'

'I'm trying to hear him breathing.'

I listened too. But all I could hear was the wild fight of my own heart. Suddenly, my thoughts flew to my dad. Was he still alive? When the Germans shot him down, did he manage to parachute out? What if this German had shot dad's plane down? Maybe Mr Scarcross was right and the only good Jerry was—

'I know he's an enemy,' Sally suddenly whispered, as though reading my thoughts. 'But he doesn't look like one.'

'He does to me,' I replied, staring at the Nazi eagle.

'Well mebbees you're not looking properly. Look at his face. You haven't looked at him properly yet, Tommy man.'

My gaze stayed on the Nazi eagle. I couldn't bring myself to look at his face. 'Sally, he's definitely a member of the Luftwaffe.'

But Sally wasn't listening. 'Enemy or not, doesn't matter,' she said. 'He's proper dead now. He's not breathing. Hasn't got nee pulse, and he—'

Sally jumped back like a salmon leaping in the beck.

'Just opened his eyes,' she gasped.

We'd never crawled back down that tunnel so quickly. Then we fled through the woods.

At the tarn, we stopped to get our breath back. A tawny owl hooted. The rising moon was spilling its silver over the tarn.

'How can I help it if he cannet make up his mind if he's dead or alive?'

'Come on,' I said.

'What do you mean?' Sally demanded.

'We'll have to tell Auntie Annie now.'

'What, in the middle of the night? And will you tell her aboot climbing doon the drainpipe an' all?'

'I don't care,' I said. 'It's too important. Anyway, the Home Guard are coming. She'll tell them when they get here. They'll obey the rules.'

'Aye,' Sally shot back. 'And what aboot old Snakecross?'

'What about him?'

Before I could reply, I felt a rush of relief: 'Look,' I cried. 'They're coming! The Home Guard.'

We could see their bike lamps. Freewheeling down the steep road into Woundale, their dynamo lights seemed to float in the night like will-o'-the-wisps.

'They're heading to ours,' I said, as the lamps began converging on our whitewashed farmhouse.

I started running. Quicker than the bats flitting over the tarn, Sally tore after me. 'Where you gannin'?' she demanded.

'We can take the Home Guard straight to the airman. Don't you see, Sally? This means everything's going to be all right. They won't shoot him. And we won't get into trouble. We can say we've just found him.'

Sally pulled me to a halt. 'Tommy man, Scarcross is in the Home Guard.'

'So what? They won't let Mr Scarcross hurt him,' I said. 'They're British. We don't shoot prisoners of war.'

'Is that what you think?' Sally said.

'Yes, it is,' I cried.

Already the bike lamps were arriving at our farmhouse. You could hear Connie barking and people shouting.

'My uncle is in the British army,' I said. 'My dad is in the RAF.'

'I know, Tommy, but—'

'Auntie Dolly's young man is in the Home Guard.'

'I'm not saying they're all bad, Tommy man, but—'

'What are you saying then?'

Suddenly, a heron that had been hunting silently on the far shore, took flight and flapped heavily away over the water. Someone was hurrying towards us from the house. A large, shambling figure took shape.

'It's Silent Simon,' said Sally.

Silent Simon was out of breath and shaking his head vigorously. When I tried to get past him, he lifted his arms wide to stop me — like you do when you're rounding up sheep.

'Let me past, Simon,' I said.

Still shaking his head, Silent Simon stretched his arms even wider.

'Trying to tell us something, isn't he?' said Sally. 'What is it, Simon?' Sally went right up to Silent Simon, and standing on her tiptoes, peered into his face. 'Is it Scarecross?'

Silent Simon nodded.

'Simon's warning us!' Sally suddenly cried. 'Quick.' And she dragged all three of us into the clump of willows growing by the tarn. This was another one of our dens. From there you could watch the path without being seen.

'What are we hiding for?' I said. 'We should be—'

I tried to step free of the trees but Sally held me back. 'Trust me,' she whispered. 'Now, whisht. They're coming this way.'

10

Hiding in the willows we could hear the drill of marching boots. The Home Guard were heading towards us. My aunties had told me never to stare at Simon, but I couldn't stop myself looking up at him now. His face was caught in the moonlight and as he listened to the approaching Home Guard, his mild brown eyes were wide with terror.

The Home Guard stopped right in front of us. I peered through the leaves. They'd only been formed a few weeks ago and didn't have uniforms yet, or proper weapons. Some carried shotguns; others just had mucking-out graips. They didn't have ranks either, but it was clear who had taken charge — and why Silent Simon was warning us.

'Right, lads,' said a familiar voice. 'Let's get sorted.'

I peered through the leaves to see Mr Scarcross.

'We'll divide into two groups,' he ordered them. 'You lads go and search around the force.'

'You see,' whispered Sally. 'Scarcross is in charge.'

I watched Mr Scarcross count off eight men.

'The rest stay here with me,' he commanded.

'Shouldn't we wait until the morning?' one of the eight men asked. 'When it's light?'

'No, we flamin' well shouldn't,' Mr Scarcross replied. 'I want him caught now. The moon's bright enough to see by. Now away you lot go.'

The first group hurried away. With them was Auntie Dolly's Stan — wearing his scarf.

'Right, lads,' Mr Scarcross said to the three remaining men. 'Now we've got rid of them wet lettuces, it's time for some sport.' He put a cigarette in his mouth and struck a match. In the flare, you could see he was enjoying himself. 'If there's a Hun here in Woundale, we're going to be the ones to make him wish he'd never been born a Jerry.'

The cigarette smoke drifted over to the willows, and Silent Simon's nose began to twitch. Sally reached out and shoved a finger under his nostrils. Just in time, Silent Simon swallowed back the sneeze.

Mr Scarcross brought out a small bottle from his pocket, took a swig and handed it round the others.

'Whisky,' Sally mouthed.

'I've searched everywhere,' Scarcross carried on. 'But if Fritz is here, he'll be likely hiding in the woods. Now this is what we're going to do. Shoot first, ask questions later. Understood, lads?' The answer was a ragged laughter. 'Shoot anything that flamin' well moves.' More laughter. Scarcross lifted his shotgun. And the others did the same. 'We know what Jerry's like, don't we, lads? We all saw enough of him in the last war. Well, he's going to see us now. Oh aye, he's going to get a right bloody good look.'

Mr Scarcross's gang marched away.

Sally turned to Silent Simon. 'That's two favours we owe you,' she whispered. 'But you've got to gan home now. Divvent follow us. Gan and stay where it's safe.'

We watched Silent Simon disappear into the night.

'How did he know to warn us?' I asked. 'How did he even know we were here?'

'Mebbees he knows what's gannin' on, bonny lad. Mebbees he knows more than folk realise.'

'How?'

'Search me. He's a deep one. Might not say much, but he knows. Now do you understand aboot Scarcross?'

I nodded.

'Him and his pals won't give the German gadgie a chance to surrender. Right come on then,' she said and, to my horror, she started off after Mr Scarcross's gang.

'Where are you going, Sal?'

'You heard Scarecrow,' she replied. 'Got to save the airman, haven't we? We left the den front door open. Scarcross will see the tunnel. They'll find him, and it'll be our fault.'

'Are you barmy?' I demanded.

'Mebbees I am. But I know one thing. Barmy or not, I'm not going to let Scarcross hurt anything else. You see, I made myself a promise. You know his barrel?'

'The water butt by the byre?'

'That's where I saw him droon the kittens.'

'Droon?'

'Aye, droon. What's the matter with you, Tommy man — cannet you speak the King's English? Twelve of them,' she explained. 'One by one. Lifted each kitten by the scruff of the neck, and held them under the water. When I tried to stop him, he said it was his duty. Said the government had told everyone to get rid of all non-working animals because of food shortages.'

'But a cat on a farm counts as a working animal,' I said. 'They catch mice and rats.'

'That's what I told him,' Sally returned. 'But he just laughed. First few kittens didn't put up nee fight. Thought he was just their mam. Cos that's how a kitten's mam carries her babies. By the scruff of the neck. Next few mewed a bit when they felt the water. The rest sort of screamed. Scarcross enjoyed that. You could tell. The way he lifted them free a few times just to make them know that he was drooning them. The sound of their crying would have broken a heart of stone, but when I tried to stop him, he knocked us doon. Said I'd be next if I ever interfered again. Soon there was only one kitten left. She knew what was happening, and she wasn't gannin' easy. Spat. Kicked. Hissed. Scratched. Must have clawed him good and proper cos he swore like a Gatesheed docker and dropped her, sucking his hand. I'm glad she did, but it didn't dee her nee good. Scarcross just put a pair of big gloves on and then came back to finish her off. Didn't see much of life, did they, Tommy man? Them kittens. Only knew a few days of sun and rain. Never went no further than the farmyard. Then there they were, floating in the water barrel like a handful of leaves. And only me to know that they'd ever been alive.'

I'd never heard Sally sound so upset before. But to my amazement, when she looked at me, the moonlight couldn't find any tears. Instead, her eyes were blazing with determination.

'That's when I made meself the promise,' she whispered. 'I swore doon that I would never let Snakecross take nee more pleasure in hurting a single other defenceless creature. Not even a German airman gadgie.'

11

Snapping twigs and tripping on brambles, smoking cigarettes, drinking and swearing, Scarcross's gang made so much noise that it was easy to find them in the woods. We followed them for a while then, when we weren't far from the old oak, Sally suddenly stopped. She listened intently for a few moments. 'This way,' she whispered, then plunged off the path.

The moon slipped behind clouds and everything went dark. Blindly, we shouldered our way through the trees; dived low under overhanging branches; waded through brambles and nettles. Finding one of the many badger paths that crisscrossed the woods, we followed it through drifts of wild garlic. Most of the garlic flowers were finished by now — but the air was still heady with the strong scent. I had no idea where Sally was taking us.

Suddenly she gripped my arm: 'Not another step, Tom.'

At that moment, the moon came back out, and I saw the Giant's Teeth. But we weren't down in the hollow. The stone circle lay beneath us. Sally had led us to the crag above the den. From up here, the tallest of the moon-splashed stones looked like the tusk of some huge, extinct animal. The whin bushes crouched thickly, guarding the German airman. Even from up here the giant's parlour was a secret. But for how much longer — 'Get down,' Sally whispered.

We ducked behind a rock. From where we hid, we could hear Scarcross and his gang walking towards the Giant's Teeth. If they looked closely enough, the moonlight would definitely show them the opening to the tunnel and the way into the giant's parlour. 'We'll have to distract them,' Sally murmured, and snatching up a couple of stones, thrust one at me. 'Bet you can't hoy it all the way over the Giant's Teeth,' she challenged.

Hoy — throw. We often had stone throwing competitions. I nodded.

'After three,' Sally whispered. 'One, two, three —'

We both threw with all our might then watched our stones sail high over the Giant's Teeth circle, and plummet into the trees beyond.

'Over there!' Scarcross shouted.

A cloud covered the moon, plunging us back into darkness. At the same moment, a ragged volley of gunfire roared out. The sparks of the Home Guard's shotguns rose on the night.

'After him, lads!' Scarcross yelled.

When the moon came out again, we saw Scarcross's gang disappearing into the woods. They'd taken the bait.

'That'll keep them busy,' Sally grinned. 'Howay.'

Sally hurried us back the way we'd come until we found

our path again. This took us the usual way to the Giant's Teeth. Quickly, we laid the branches back, concealing the mouth of the tunnel.

'What now?' I asked.

'Now we skedaddle,' she said.

'What about the airman?' I asked.

Sally didn't reply. We ran to the tarn.

'What about the German gadgie?' I repeated.

'I thought you understood,' Sally said.

'But we can't just leave him there.'

'Well, that's where you're wrong. Because that's exactly what we are going to dee. For tonight, anyway.'

'It's a crime not to report an enemy combatant.'

'And it's a crime to let Stinkcross shoot a helpless man. We've got to look after him, Tom. Just until we can get him safely surrendered. Now, are you going to help me or not?'

My head span. I honestly didn't know what to do.

Closing my eyes tight, I wondered what my dad would advise if he were here. Now, I needed him more than ever. Then I remembered one of the last conversations we'd had, just before he left to join the RAF. I'd said that all Germans were bad and he should kill as many as he could. But he'd shaken his head, and told me that no country was all bad. People were people, he said. He said that under the uniform every German was just like us. They were all somebody's brother, somebody's son — somebody's father.

Somebody's father. The words he had spoken resounded

in my head now. I nodded. 'All right,' I whispered. 'I'll help. Just until we can get him safely surrendered.'

Sally grinned. 'Knew you would, Tommy. Now, we'll both have to promise — nee blabbing.' Reaching deep into the pocket of her kecks, Sally held out what looked like a fistful of dirty rags. 'Take this,' she urged. 'And give your word that you'll keep your trap shut. Swear doon not to tell aboot the secret of our German airman.'

I took the rags. It was only now that the moonlight showed me what it was. Worn out, in tatters — a rag doll.

'Raise her in your right hand,' Sally ordered.

'This is stupid.'

'Divvent call Tilly stupid.' Sally's eyes narrowed. 'Hold her higher and repeat after me: I, Thomas Grisedale ...'

'You know, who I am,' I protested.

'I, Thomas Grisedale,' she repeated.

'I, Thomas Grisedale.'

'Mainly known as, Tommy.'

'Mainly known as, Tommy.'

'Of Woundale Farm.'

'Get on with it,' I protested.

'Of Woundale Farm,' Sally repeated.

'Of Woundale Farm,' I echoed.

'In the back of beyond.'

'I'm not saying that.'

Sally grinned. 'In the middle of Lakeland.'

'In the middle of Lakeland.'

'Do solemnly swear . . .'

'Do solemnly swear . . .'

'To keep the secret of the German gadgie with me, Sally Smith.'

'To keep the secret of the German gadgie with me, Sally Smith.'

'You're not Sally Smith,' snapped Sally. 'You did that on purpose, you great big country bumpkin.'

'To keep the secret of the German gadgie with you, Sally Smith,' I repeated.

Sally grinned again. 'We'll soon have you talking proper.' But the grin quickly disappeared. Now Sally was staring at me so intently that I had to look away. She always won the staring competitions. 'You've sworn, Tommy,' she said. 'You cannet gan back on it, mind.'

'I won't.'

'If you do, your tongue will turn into an eel, and your heart will fly away like a cuckoo — and not never find its way back. And I'll never talk to you again. Agreed?'

'Agreed.'

'Champion. We're in it together.'

'Your turn,' I said.

'I've already sworn,' she said. 'Right, there's nowt more we can dee tonight. But divvent worry, Tommy man, you saw for yourself he won't be gannin' neewhere soon. He must have crawled to that den like an injured animal. He'll be safe there for tonight. I'll work out what to dee by tomorrow.

I'll come up with a plan. You'll see. Now howay, you'd better get home before them aunties of yours think you've been kidnapped.'

'What about you?'

'What aboot me?'

'What if Scarcross finds out what we're doing?'

'I can handle him,' Sally shot back. 'Told you before. I look after meself. Divvent need nee help from neebody, me. Never have. Never will.'

TAN ...

1

I didn't realise how tired I was until I got into bed. I must have fallen asleep immediately because the next thing I knew, morning was glimmering at the blackout curtains and Connie was slurping me awake with her long tongue. Connie was my alarm clock. Even when she slept outside, she was always allowed in to wake me up. A minute later, Auntie Annie was calling me for breakfast.

I unhooked the blackout curtains, and the bright morning light flowed in. The farmyard was dotted with hens. Mouser, our ginger tabby cat, was sleeping in the sun. Our few milk cows grazed in their field along with their calves. A breeze ruffled the tarn. The cuckoo called from the bulrushes. Across the water stood the Scarcross place. And clinging thickly to the dale side above us all — the woods. Deep green with early summer, they were hiding a Nazi.

The grandfather clock was chiming as I came down the stairs. Five o'clock. We always got up a little bit earlier on Sundays. We had to do our morning jobs before chapel. There were no rest days during the war. But at least it was light; in winter the early mornings were pitch black.

Auntie Annie handed me a bowl of porridge from the pot on the range. I joined the others at the table.

'I still think he's out there somewhere,' Auntie Gladys said, whispering so Auntie Annie didn't hear.

'Well, Mr Scarcross and the Home Guard didn't find anything,' murmured Auntie Dolly as she helped Vi to eat her porridge. Though Vi was Auntie Gladys's daughter, my other aunties treated her like their own. Like they did with me. 'Stan told me when he came to the door just now,' Auntie Dolly went on. 'Apparently, Mr Scarcross thought they had found him, but it was only a deer.'

My stomach lurched.

'How do you want your egg, Tommy?' Auntie Annie asked.

'I had one yesterday,' I replied, trying to make my voice sound as normal as possible.

Because of the war we were only supposed to have one egg a week. The rest were carted to town. As Auntie Annie said, we all have to make sacrifices for the war effort.

'You deserve an extra one,' Auntie Dolly said.

'You've been working hard,' said Auntie Gladys.

Auntie Annie nodded. 'You need your strength, lad. You're not far off from doing a man's job now.'

I blushed at the thought of the neglected tattie patch. 'Scrambled please,' I said, before suddenly remembering: 'Actually, may I have it hardboiled, for later?' This way Sally could share it. I'd slip it to her on the way to chapel whilst she told me about the plan to get the airman into safe custody.

'I've put your clothes out ready for chapel,' Auntie Annie told me.

'Are you really sure we should be going to chapel, Annie?' Auntie Dolly asked.

'Why ever not?' Auntie Annie demanded. 'We always go.'

'It's just with the airman still on the loose,' said Auntie Gladys. 'What if he breaks into the house when we're away?'

'And hides upstairs, waiting for us to come back,' said Auntie Dolly.

'If there's a German airman wandering fancy free in Woundale,' said Auntie Annie. 'I'll eat our Tommy's cap.'

'But the postman said,' began Auntie Dolly and Gladys together.

'Anything but his prayers,' Auntie Annie interrupted. 'Oh, for pity's sake, there is no airman. The poor soul probably perished with the rest of the crew — or he's halfway back to Germany by now.'

Auntie Gladys and Dolly looked at their older sister. Then at each other. Then they nodded. Auntie Annie was always right.

I finished my porridge, slipped the boiled egg into my pocket and went out onto the yard. Before I could talk to Sally, I had the milking to do. Connie was waiting. Together we let the 'mams' out of their field and took them to the byre. The 'mams' were what we called the cows that had suckling calves. There were three of them: Daisy, Clover and Buttercup — gentle beasts, their soft, shaggy flanks were white with strawberry-coloured spots. Even when I had to shut the gate on their calves, the 'mams' only lowed softly. They knew that they wouldn't be away from them for long.

You must be careful milking cows with calves. You can't just empty their udders; you need to leave enough milk for the little ones. And you can't hurry them either. As I sat on the milking stool in our byre, pulling the teats and listening to the milk squirt into the pails, I kept picturing the German airman lying in the giant's parlour. Maybe he'd died. He'd looked badly injured. When I was finished, I poured the milk carefully into a churn. We always took a churn of milk to town on a Sunday morning.

Next, Connie and I took the 'mams' back to the field, opened the gate and let the calves come out. Then we led them all down to the tarn to drink, the calves frisking and frolicking as we went. It seemed impossible to believe that the war had reached Woundale.

Standing in the shallows of the tarn, the cows drank deeply. As the water streamed from their mouths, the sun turned the droplets into sparkling diamonds. Red damselflies glinted as they flew round the white water crowfoot flowers that carpeted this part of the tarn. Once the cattle had drunk their fill, I took them back to the field.

'Thomas?' Auntie Annie's voice rose from the back door as I came onto the yard.

'Just a tick!' I called.

No time for weeding the tatties this morning, I had to turn the fodder beet pile. I hated that job. Our sheep were up on the fells, but they'd be coming down for shearing soon, and the fodder beet had to be kept as rat free as possible, for them to eat. We couldn't keep rats away completely, but if you forked over the beet pile, moving it and restacking it, you would disturb the rodents, and prevent them from nesting. Rats don't like being disturbed. This morning, only half a dozen ran over my boots and shot away. Hearing the sound, Mouser appeared from nowhere.

'Tommy, make sure you wash your hands and face before chapel,' Auntie Annie called from the back door. 'And not just a cat's lick today.'

'Just doing it now,' I replied, running to the pump on the yard.

Gasping at the cold water, I took the soap from its little tin box, and closing my eyes against the suds, washed my face.

When I could open my eyes again, I saw Auntie Annie coming towards me. Her headscarf had gone, and in its place was her black Sunday beret. She always wore a plain, black woollen dress for chapel. And a silver chain. On the chain was her wedding ring. At least, it would have been her wedding ring, if her fiancé hadn't been killed in the last war. He'd signed up on the first day of hostilities with the local 'Pals Battalion', like everyone else round here. They'd all joined up together. Auntie Annie's fiancé had only been in France for a week when a German shell had exploded in his trench, killing him and five of his Lakeland pals in one go. Every Sunday, Auntie Annie wore the unused ring round her neck in memory of what had never been.

'When was the last time you ran this through that lovely red hair of yours, Thomas Grisedale?' Auntie Annie asked, holding up her Sunday comb.

'Last Sunday, by the looks of it,' laughed Auntie Gladys as she and Vi collected the eggs. Auntie Gladys was dressed for chapel too, in a green dress and hat to match. The hat looked like a bowl of pea soup upturned on her head. Vi had a red ribbon in her hair.

'Here, make friends with this,' Auntie Annie said, taking out the nail brush from the soap tin. She began scrubbing my fingernails.

'Mr Scarcross is coming!' shouted Auntie Gladys. 'Hurry up, everyone.'

We always travelled to town on Sunday with Scarcross. Come rain, come shine (and sometimes, hail and snow) both farmhouses made the journey together in Scarcross's cart.

Auntie Dolly and I rushed to carry the churn out of the byre. We had to be extra careful not to splash any milk. As well as having her hair rolled with an extra curl, Auntie Dolly was wearing her best blue and white polka dot Sunday frock. We put the churns beside the egg trays, ready to be loaded onto the back of the cart.

'You going to chapel dressed like that, Tommy?' Auntie Annie asked.

I hadn't changed out of my work clothes yet.

I sprinted upstairs. My shirt was waiting on a hanger. My jumper and cloth cap were set on the dresser, by the framed photograph. All my Sunday best had been made by my aunties, except for my tweed jacket. I was very proud of that jacket. It had been my dad's when he was a boy. Each Sunday as I put it on, for a moment he seemed to be standing beside me again.

'Thomas!' All three aunties seemed to shout at the same time as I came hurtling downstairs, tying my woollen tie, my cap just managing to cling to my head.

Reaching the door, I realised that I'd forgotten to polish everyone's Sunday shoes. That was another of my jobs since my dad had left. I was supposed to make them shine so you could see your face in them.

'Don't worry,' winked Auntie Dolly, handing me my brown leather shoes. 'I polished them all this morning.'

'Champion,' I grinned.

'He's here!' Auntie Gladys cried.

I could hear Arnold pulling Scarcross's cart onto our yard. Then: 'Rag and bone!' Sally's voice rang out. 'Any old rags and bones?'

As I hurried out of the house, I couldn't believe what I was seeing. There was no sign of Scarcross. Sally was standing up at the front of the cart, holding Arnold's reins. Scarcross never let anyone else drive his cart.

2

'Mr Scarcross cannet come this morning,' Sally announced. 'He's otherwise engaged.'

Auntie Gladys and Auntie Dolly stared, open mouthed.

Silent Simon was sitting beside Sally. They were both grinning away. Silent Simon was doffing his Sunday bowler hat. Sally had put a daisy chain round it. 'Aye,' nodded Sally. 'The Home Guard have been ordered to search the far side of Dead Man's Pike. Someone said they thought they saw a parachute over there when the bomber flew over.'

Dead Man's Pike was a mountain on the far side of town.

'You'd best get down from there,' Auntie Annie ordered. 'Mr Scarcross wouldn't want us taking his cart without him.'

'But what about the milk,' said Sally. 'And the eggs?' Sally and Silent Simon had already loaded the Scarcross milk churns and egg baskets onto the back of the cart, leaving space for ours. 'We can't just leave them here. There's a war on, you know. And we can't carry them to town ourselves.'

'She's right, Annie,' Auntie Gladys said.

'The Ministry of Food won't want all this lot gannin' to waste,' said Sally.

Auntie Annie nodded. 'But I'd better drive, lass,' she said. 'It's not easy handling a cart on the fells.'

Sally and Silent Simon jumped down, and we lifted the churn and eggs onto the back of the cart.

Auntie Annie had climbed up and taken the reins. She clicked her tongue gently and Arnold set off. The rest of us always walked the first part of the journey, to save Arnold on the steep road lifting out of Woundale.

As the cart trundled up the slope, Auntie Dolly and Gladys followed it, swinging Vi along between them. Silent Simon played with Connie, throwing a stick for her to fetch. With Scarcross not here, it was like a holiday. Sally and I dropped behind. She didn't have any Sunday best. She was in her 'land girl kecks' but she wore a brand-new mustard-coloured cardigan knitted for her by Auntie Annie. And her black hair was tied into a pony tail with some of Vi's red ribbon.

'Areet, bonny lass,' I said, using one of her Geordie greetings.

'Gan and take a long walk off a short pier,' she returned.

'Find yourself a friendly cliff,' I replied.

'And see if you can fly,' we both said at the same time, then grinned. We often greeted each other with insults, Sally said it was the normal way on Tyneside.

'Here,' I said, passing Sally the egg I had saved from breakfast.

'Champion,' she grinned.

Sally opened her mouth to bite into it. Then seemed to change her mind.

'You first,' she said, thrusting the egg back at me.

I shook my head. 'You need it more than I do.'

'Remember what we agreed, Tommy man. I'll only take things, if you have half.'

'I already have,' I said. 'I got two eggs this morning.'

'Tommy Grisedale, divvent fib.'

'I'm not fibbing,' I said, crossing my fingers behind my back.

'Honest?'

'Cross my heart.'

Giving a wink, Sally suddenly tossed the boiled egg high in the air. Catching it in her mouth, she bit it into two, then bulged her cheeks like a hamster — half an egg in each side. I burst into laughter. With a chomp and a grin, she swallowed it down.

'So did you come up with one?' I asked.

'With what?'

'A plan?'

'Why aye. Course I have, Tommy man.'

'What is it then?'

'I'll tell you after chapel. But I've been thinking, Tommy. You divvent have to help us. With your dad and everything. I'll help the German gadgie by meself, if it bothers you.'

'But isn't your dad fighting somewhere as well, Sal?'

As usual, she didn't answer. Instead, she said: 'Do you think he's a dad? I mean, the German gadgie.'

Now it was my turn not to answer. 'What if he's part of an invading force? What if he's hiding a military communication transmitting device?'

'What's that in English?'

'A radio.'

'He hasn't got nee radio.'

'He might have one hidden somewhere.'

'Oh aye; where — in his boots?'

'He could easily conceal a listening device in his coverall pockets. If he's got signalling equipment, during an invasion he could contact other Nazis.'

Before we could discuss it further, Auntie Annie was calling: 'All aboard!' — we'd climbed out of Woundale and reached the fells.

'Just think,' said Auntie Dolly, as she lifted Vi into the cart. 'We'll be seeing that Nazi plane for ourselves soon.'

'There won't be much to see,' said Auntie Annie. 'Just a pile of wreckage.'

'Won't it be dangerous?' Auntie Gladys replied. 'I mean, what if there are unexploded bombs?'

'I expect everything that was going to explode, exploded when it crash-landed,' said Auntie Annie. 'Giddy up,' she called to Arnold, lifting the reins.

It was a beautiful, sunny morning. The mountain air was as fresh as spring water. White bog cotton shimmered in the heather. The skylarks sang as though they didn't know how to stop.

I loved being up on the fells. From here, mountain peak after mountain peak stretched as far as the eye could see. Connie ran happily alongside us. Silent Simon sat up front with Auntie Annie. Auntie Dolly and Auntie Gladys sat in the main part of the cart with Vi. And Sally and I perched amongst the milk churns and eggs at the back, our legs dangling over as though we were sitting right at the top of the world.

'Tyneside's that way,' I said to Sally, pointing over the mountains.

'How do you know?' she demanded.

'It's north east.'

She shrugged. 'Aren't you the clever one.'

'Don't you miss it at all?' I asked.

'What, miss being back there?'

I nodded.

'Would you miss having a hole in your heed?' she snapped, still gazing in the opposite direction. 'Not to mention so much smoke you cannet breathe proper.'

Just then, Auntie Annie began to sing 'Amazing Grace'. We all joined in. Our voices seemed to mingle with the songs of the skylarks as they rose higher and higher. I tried to picture Tyneside. All those streets, the smoke, the pits. I knew we got our coal from Tyneside, and that there was a big river there too — the Tyne. But I didn't know anything else.

'Next hymn is "Abide with Me",' Auntie Annie announced.

In time we reached the fast-flowing beck with its high humped bridge. Here we all got out again, so that Arnold didn't have to heft us all over the bridge. After the bridge was the crossroads with its four-ways signpost.

'That reminds me,' said Auntie Dolly. 'Stan told me we've got to change all the signs round. So, the Germans won't know which way to go.'

'There's more than one German here now, is there?' snapped Auntie Annie.

'I don't just mean the airman,' said Auntie Dolly. 'Stan said it was a government order. In case—'

'Of an invasion,' Auntie Gladys finished for her. 'You see, when the invasion begins, we have to confuse them. Send them the wrong way. Away from towns.'

We all looked up at the familiar crossroads sign. The four large fingerposts rose above us, each pointing in a different direction.

'We'll need a ladder to get up there,' Auntie Annie muttered.

'Who needs a ladder?' Sally giggled as she jumped down from the cart and began shinnying her way up.

'Come down, before you fall, lass,' said Auntie Annie.

'It's easier than a drainpipe,' Sally called back.

And my aunties burst into laughter. I forced myself to grin, and hoped she wouldn't say anything more.

At the top, Sally pushed the finger posts round.

'Now all the Germans will come to Woundale,' Auntie Dolly said.

'Then we really would have to start locking the door at night,' smiled Auntie Annie.

'And if they want to go to Windermere,' said Auntie Gladys, reading the names of the other places on the crossroads way markers, 'they'll end up in Seascale.'

'Is Seascale the seaside?' Sally called from the top of the sign.

'Aye, but it'll take you a while to get there,' said Auntie Gladys. 'It's yon end of the fells.'

Whistling 'Oh, I Do Like to Be Beside the Seaside' through the gap in her teeth, Sally slid back down like a fireman on a pole.

At last, town came into view — a steep hillside of stone cottages, half a dozen shops and pubs, the granite-grey church rising above it all, like a great crag. Our chapel was the far smaller red-brick building, standing to one side of the village. But none of us were looking at churches or chapels this morning. Everyone in the cart had stood up, and was craning their neck towards the churchyard, trying to get a view of the German bomber. The plane had landed in the part of the churchyard nearest the school. Smashed headstones lay all around.

A crowd was gathered round what was left of the plane. Everybody in the whole town seemed to be there, gazing at the wreckage — and from far and wide too. Nothing like this had ever happened before.

With a sudden laugh of excitement, Sally jumped from the still-moving cart and ran to the crowd. I followed. And so did Connie.

3

'Keep close, Tommy man,' Sally said, as she wriggled through the throng, working her way to the front. No one seemed to notice us; everyone was too busy staring at the plane, discussing why it had crashed here.

'Engine failure,' someone was saying.

'No, it deliberately tried to crash into the church,' another claimed.

'Was aiming for the houses,' a third person added.

'Or wanted to hit the school,' said a fourth.

Auntie Annie had been wrong. There was a lot to see. Fuselage blackened from the explosion, wide wings snapped off, the German bomber plane lay massive amongst the tombstones. The propellers poked up like giant ribs.

I nodded to myself: 'Heinkel He 111.'

'Like a dragon,' Sally murmured to herself. 'A burned oot dragon, with its wings singed off.'

I recognised most of the crowd. Both of our teachers were there — nice Miss Jameson, and Miss Gently who was anything but gentle. The butcher, Mr Tupperman; Mrs Bell, the baker's wife; Mr Conway, a publican; and Mr Musgrove, the veterinary surgeon. Mr Rebanks the shepherd was also there, with his long white hair, tall weathered crook and two border collies. Stan's brothers were there too. Even Sergeant Collinson, the town bobby, was gawping with the rest, right at the front.

Most of the children from school were there as well, including the other evacuees. Bertie Tupperman, the butcher's son, had got the best view. Bertie Tupperman, a foot taller than everyone else. Bertie Tupperman, the school bully. 'Look what the cat's brought in,' I heard him say. 'The Geordie stinker is here.'

Bertie Tupperman hated Sally. Everyone else tried to keep in his good books, or out of his way, but she never did. Everyone else laughed at his jokes, but she never did. Everyone else was terrified of him, but she wasn't.

'Thought I could smell something,' he continued. 'Hold your noses.'

As usual, Sally quietened him straight away: 'Look who it isn't,' she shot back. 'Squirty Butterman.'

You could tell he was angry, but frightened that she might say something even worse. Sally always won the insults competition. Ignoring Bertie Tupperman, she was staring at the plane wreckage. 'What's that bit, Tommy?' she whispered, pointing at the large, buckled frame of metal and glass. 'Looks like one of them huts made out of glass.'

'A greenhouse?'

She nodded.

'It's the navigator's turret,' I said. 'It goes right at the front, under the pilot. So he gets a good view.'

'You mean, the German gadgie was sitting in that greenhouse, thousands of feet up?'

I looked around uneasily, in case anyone had overheard. But no one had. The verger was calling everyone in to church. Before the war, the church bells had summoned the congregation, but that wasn't allowed now. All over the country, church bells could only be rung to warn of the invasion. Immediately the crowd began melting away. Miss Gently led the way. She glared at Sally as she passed us. Miss Gently didn't like Sally either. The other evacuees scampered away too. They never talked to Sally, and she never talked to them. 'Why don't you go back to where you belong?' Bertie Tupperman said as he walked past Sally. 'We don't want no thieving townies round here.'

'Go back, go back, go back to where you belong,' she sang back. 'Go back to the land of Bertie Tupperpong.'

Soon only we chapel-goers were left around the plane. Our service started a quarter of an hour later than the one in the big church.

'Imagine, how many bombs would fit in that,' said Auntie Dolly. 'Enough to blow up half of Woundale.'

'It was on a recce,' remarked one of the soldiers guarding the wreckage, not a Home Guard but a real soldier. 'You know, a reconnaissance flight.'

'What's one of them?' Sally asked.

'Jerry bombers have been mapping out where all the shipyards and factories are for when the bombing starts,' he explained. 'This one was looking for Barrow most likely. Must have got lost.'

'Lost?' put in Auntie Gladys.

'And no wonder,' said the soldier. 'There doesn't seem to have been a navigator. Unless he really did parachute out like everyone's been saying.'

'Time for chapel,' Auntie Annie called, already at the church gate.

'I knew it,' Sally whispered to me as my aunties made for our little red brick chapel.

'Knew what?'

'Knew he was a good enemy.'

'How can you have a good enemy?' I asked.

'He parachuted oot so Hitler wouldn't know where to drop all them bombs.' And with that she ran to the gate.

4

After the service, Auntie Annie checked that the milk and eggs had all been collected by the Ministry of Food, and that the empty churns and trays had been returned. Then she drove us back to Woundale — or to the town, as the signpost now said.

When we'd reached the uneven stretch of road where the rumble of the wheels would safely drown out our voices, I turned to Sally: 'So what's your plan?'

'Guess who this is, Tommy,' she demanded, then pulled a straining face and groaned.

'Who?'

'Scarcross on the privy,' she laughed.

'I'm asking about the plan.'

'Oh, I thought you meant pan — you kna, the toilet pan.'

'Be serious, Sally. You said you had a plan.'

'Course I dee. But tell us something first. What are those little bushes?'

I followed her pointing finger to the low growing bushes that filled a whole fell side.

'Bilberries,' I said.

'Bilberries; can you eat them?'

I nodded. 'In a week or two, those bushes will be full of berries. We'll pick them.'

'Are you allowed to?' she asked in wonder.

I shrugged. 'No one owns them. They belong to everyone.'

'Are they nice?'

'They're champion.'

We both grinned.

'We'll come and get a load in a fortnight, Tommy.'

I liked seeing Woundale and the fells through Sally's eyes. I'd never really understood how special they were until I got to share them like this. And as the cart rumbled across the fells, for a while I was just happy to gaze at it all. The war seemed very far away. The invasion, and even the hiding airman, seemed to be happening in a different world.

Only it wasn't happening in a different world. It was happening here. Happening to us. And I needed to know what we were going to do.

'So what is it then?' I whispered to Sally as we got off the cart to walk up the humpback bridge.

'What's what?' she replied, gazing over the parapet at the rushing beck.

'Your plan.'

She tapped her nose. 'I'll tell you later. Are you sure that anyone can just scran all them bilberries?'

'Stop blethering about bilberries, Sal,' I insisted. 'I need to know our plan now.'

At that moment the cart lurched as it went over a pothole on the bridge, making the empty milk churns rattle. I felt my stomach do the same — all at once I realised why Sally wasn't telling me her plan: 'You haven't got one, have you, Sally? You don't know what to do.'

'Course I have,' she shot back, 'and for your information, it's the best plan I've ever had.'

'Then why don't you just tell me what it is?'

'Why, why, dog cack pie,' she chanted. 'Just because you know about Luftwaffe pistols and bilberries doesn't mean you know everything. Besides, we can't dee anything until this afternoon anyway. We've got all our jobs to dee first. And then there's Sunday School.'

This was true. There were more jobs to do when we got back, followed by Sunday dinner, and after that Sunday School. It wasn't a proper Sunday School, it was what Sally called the extra lessons that Auntie Annie gave us every Sunday afternoon, to make up for the ones we had to miss when farm work or bad weather prevented us getting to school. Scarcross had tried to stop our Sunday School, but Auntie Annie had insisted. Before my mam had died, Auntie Annie had been a teacher. She'd given it up to look after me.

'I'll tell you the plan after Sunday School,' Sally said.

'So, we're just going to leave him in the giant's parlour until then?' I asked, as we jumped back into the cart.

'Divvent worry, Tom, he likes being there.'

'How do you know?' I queried, speaking so loudly that for a moment I thought the others might have heard me.

'Told me, didn't he?' Sally returned.

'You've spoken to him?'

'Divvent snap at us, man. I took him some breakfast this morning. What was I supposed to dee — let him starve?'

'And he speaks English?'

'Well he didn't actually say anything, but he smiled when he opened his eyes. And kept nodding. Then he just lay back and went to sleep, so I put the scran doon for him, and left.'

5

As Auntie Annie drove Sally and Silent Simon back in the cart to Scarcross's farm, I went into our byre and began chopping the week's firewood for the cooking range. With each chop of the axe, I thought it was the sound of the airman coming onto the yard. How could all of this be happening? The worst of it was, I didn't think Sally knew what we were going to do. And neither did I.

Before I'd finished, I was being called in for the best meal of the week. A mountain of tatties was waiting, with Yorkshire puds, cabbage, kale and even a small piece of pork. Just to smell it, made you feel like a king. And the best part of it all was that Sally could enjoy it too. As well as the lessons, Auntie Annie always kept a plate of Sunday dinner for her. As I ate, I could see Sally's plate keeping warm on the range — she came to ours after she'd done some more jobs for Scarcross.

After our dinner, my aunties washed the dishes, and I went out to finish chopping the wood. And to wait for Sally. But for some reason, she was late in coming today. Surely she hadn't gone to see the airman again?

'Mr Scarcross is right about one thing,' I overheard Auntie Gladys saying as I carried a heavy armful of logs into the house. 'Wilder than a weasel is exactly what she is.' Hovering in the hall, I listened. 'The way she was driving that cart,' Auntie Gladys went on. 'Her, just a slip of a lass. And did you see how she climbed up the signpost? Where did she learn tricks like that?'

'Weren't you young yourself, once, Glad?' Auntie Annie said.

'What about the way she eats,' Auntie Gladys continued. 'Can barely use a knife and fork. What kind of home has she come from?'

'Postman said she's never written a single letter home,' Auntie Dolly pointed out. 'Or got one.'

'Not everyone can read and write, Doll,' said Auntie Annie. 'Sally struggled herself when she first arrived. Maybe her mam and dad never learnt how to.'

'We don't even know for certain that she's a proper evacuee,' put in Auntie Gladys.

'What on earth do you mean by that?' Auntie Annie demanded.

Auntie Gladys dropped her voice: 'There's been talk.'

'What talk?' said Auntie Annie. 'If it's that flaming postman . . .'

'You know Betty Braithwaite?' said Auntie Gladys. 'I was chatting to her after chapel today. Well, her cousin is on the evacuee committee, and she said that they've had all sorts of trouble with runaways.'

Auntie Annie bristled. 'Sally's no runaway. The lass has been here since last autumn.'

'But what about before she came here?' Auntie Gladys returned. 'Betty said that it was chaos during the evacuation, with loads of bairns slipping through the net. She said that there have been cases of kids who were unhappy or in trouble at home, using the evacuation to run away. In fact, the authorities have started trying to track them down. Betty said that when she saw Sally jump from our cart, that was the first thing she thought — that girl's one of them; she's a runaway.'

'I've heard there are more bairns running in the other direction, trying to get back home because they're so poorly treated,' retorted Auntie Annie.

At that moment, one of the logs I was carrying became dislodged and nearly dropped.

'Apparently,' Auntie Gladys went on, 'they've found some sort of irregularity with Sally's paperwork.'

'She didn't have an evacuee tag when she arrived, did she?' Auntie Dolly said.

Auntie Gladys shook her head. 'Nor a gas mask. All evacuees were given a gas mask.'

'As if she'd need one in Woundale,' returned Auntie Annie. 'And as for a label, well we know who she is.'

'Do we?' Auntie Gladys continued. 'The truth is, we don't rightly know where she's from.'

'Tyneside,' Auntie Annie returned. 'Just listen to the way she talks. She's as Geordie as a pit pony.'

'Yes, but whereabouts on Tyneside?' Auntie Gladys asked. 'Tyneside's not like Woundale. You could fit all the folk of Cumberland and Westmorland in it and still have room for the sheep and cattle. Evacuee? What if she is one of these runaways.'

'The lass is a bit wild,' said Auntie Dolly. 'I'll give you that, but her heart's in the right place, Glad.'

'Mr Scarcross was saying that she steals,' Auntie Gladys continued. 'Nothing more than a thief, that's what he says.'

'Wouldn't you take an egg now and again if you were half-starved?' Auntie Annie demanded.

'You know what else folks are saying, don't you?' Auntie Gladys said. 'We shouldn't let our Tommy play with her.'

'I'm surprised at you, our Gladys,' returned Auntie Annie. 'Picking on a defenceless lass.'

'All I'm saying,' replied Auntie Gladys, 'is are we sure she's a good influence on our Tommy?'

'A good influence?' Auntie Annie demanded. 'Since our Arthur went missing, the only time I ever hear Tommy laughing is when he's with Sally.'

At that moment the log finally fell. I had to pretend to be just coming in.

'Lesson time now, Thomas,' Auntie Annie declared as she tied the top knot of her headscarf. She'd taken off her beret and chain for another week, and with it the never-used wedding ring. 'Your books are on the table. Make a start by copying out the poem on page twenty-three — in your best handwriting.'

Auntie Annie always made sure that I was busy when Sally came. Just like she always set a chair outside, and made sure she was waiting there with the plate of dinner when Sally arrived. Sally never ate her meal in front of anyone else. As Auntie Gladys said — she could barely use a knife and fork.

'I wonder where she is,' said Auntie Annie, after I'd written out the poem. 'It's not like her to be late for her Sunday School. I hope that Mr Scarcross isn't punishing her for taking the cart. I'll have to go round and tell him that it was my decision to take it.' She shook her head. 'It's never sat right with me, that bairn having to work for a man like him.'

'Well there's nowt more we can do about that,' said Auntie Gladys. 'We've offered to have her live with us. Even said we'd feed her to spare him the expense, but he wouldn't have it. You can't interfere in other folks' business, Annie. She's his evacuee.'

At last, I heard Auntie Annie greeting Sally in the hall. 'Hello, love. You're just in time. We've got some spare food that wants eating up. Tell you what, why don't you have it? Just sit out here, if you like. You'd be doing us a favour.'

Strange to say, it seemed that sometimes, lies could be more honest than the truth.

6

After eating her dinner, Sally came in. She was carrying her satchel. Although it wasn't proper school, she always brought her satchel. She seemed very proud of it. It had been the only thing she had fetched with her to Woundale. Opening it now, she lifted out her treasured possessions — the exercise book and Lakeland pencil Auntie Annie had given her — and sat down with me at the kitchen table.

'Will you read today's poem for us, Sally?' Auntie Annie asked, showing her the page in the book.

Sally nodded and read the poem. It was called: 'I Wandered Lonely as a Cloud'.

'Shall I read it again, Miss Grisedale?' she asked once she'd finished it. 'Because a good poem is like a mountain, once you've climbed all the way to the top, you can't just climb straight back down. You've got to spend some time enjoying the view.'

Auntie Annie smiled and nodded — these were her own words. Sally always remembered what Auntie Annie taught us. 'Yes, please, Sally,' said Auntie Annie. 'Read it again.'

'I wandered lonely as a cloud,' Sally began again. 'That floats on high o'er vales and hills . . .'

'What's a vale?' Auntie Annie asked.

'A valley?' I said.

Auntie Annie nodded.

'Same as a dale, isn't it?' said Sally. 'Like Woundale?'

Auntie Annie smiled. 'Exactly. This poem was written very near here. Carry on, Sally.'

'When all at once I saw a crowd,' Sally continued:

'A host, of golden daffodils;

'Beside the lake, beneath the trees,

'Fluttering and dancing in the breeze.'

When Sally had first come to Woundale, she could barely read at all. And now, listen to her. You'd think she was the poet.

'What's happening in the poem?' Auntie Annie asked.

'He's going for walk,' I said.

'Who is?' Auntie Annie asked.

'The poet,' I replied.

'What does he do on his walk?' Auntie Annie asked.

'Sees loads of daffodils,' I said. 'And likes them.'

'Mebbees it's more than that,' Sally said softly.

Auntie Annie nodded encouragingly.

'I mean, Miss Grisedale,' Sally continued. 'The poet's lonely. Like a cloud. You know, as though she feels faraway. As though she doesn't belong neewhere. As though she just gets blown around from place to place, like a lost airman.'

'How do you know it's a girl?' I asked, to stop her mentioning anything else about an airman.

Sally shrugged. 'It's who you want it to be, isn't it?'

'Why does she like the daffodils?' queried Auntie Annie.

Sally smiled. 'Everybody does. When I first saw them growing here, I thought somebody had robbed a bank and scattered all the gold. They were just stalks at first, and when Tommy told me they'd soon turn into gold, I thought he was pulling me leg. But then they did. He knows everything about Woundale, does Tommy. You teach us poems and numbers, Auntie Annie, and he teaches us about the flowers, birds, animals and Luftwaffe Luger pistols.'

'And the bilberries,' I put in quickly. 'We're going to collect them when they're ready.'

Auntie Annie smiled. Then poured Sally some milk. We always had a cup of milk each during Sunday's lesson. 'I thought we'd do something different today. Would you like to write a letter home, Sally?'

For a moment, Sally seemed uncertain. Her eyes darted about, like a deer when it scents danger. Then she grinned. 'What, write a letter to them back there?'

'If you'd like to.'

'No, thanks, Miss Grisedale. Can we do our sums now?'

Sally was always good at sums. But unlike at school with Miss Gently, we'd often laugh as we did them. 'Say you bought three pounds of carrots at tuppence ha'penny a pound,' Auntie Annie began. 'And then you bought a hundredweight of tatties at thruppence a pound. How much would that cost all together?'

'Too flippin' much,' said Sally. 'I'd gan to a different greengrocer me. Besides, you'd need a couple of wheelbarrows to cart all them spuds home.'

Then she began whistling the 'Potato Pete' song that we often heard on the wireless at school. We sang the song together:

'Potato Pete, Potato Pete
Look who's coming down the street . . .'

At the end of the lesson, when she was packing away her pencil and book, Sally suddenly asked: 'Auntie Annie, what's an Alleyman?'

'You what, love?'

'An Alleyman,' Sally repeated. 'What's one of them? Is it someone who lives down an alley?'

'No,' said Auntie Annie.

'What is it then?'

'An Alleyman,' Auntie Annie explained, 'is a German.'

Sally's eyes widened. 'A German?'

'At least that's what our lads called them in the last war,' said Auntie Annie.

'Like Fritz or Jerry or Hun?'

Auntie Annie nodded. 'It's French for a German — Allemand. Our lads said Alleyman. Why do you ask?'

But Sally was already at the door. I followed her outside. She was sprinting away towards the tarn.

'What came over her?' Auntie Annie asked, joining me.

'I don't know,' I said, trying to make my voice sound normal.

For a while we both stood there, watching Sally running back to the Scarcross farm. 'All alone in the world,' I heard Auntie Annie say to herself. Then, 'Tommy, does she ever tell you what it's like living at the Scarcross place?'

'Not really,' I said. And that was the truth.

Auntie Annie sighed softly. 'We're going to have to start looking after Sally,' she said, reaching up to tie her headscarf knot a little tighter. 'Right, while you're out here, will you cut some dandelions for the mams? We need to get a bit more milk out of them to give to that lass.'

I nodded. Cows love dandelions.

'Get the leaves,' Auntie Annie continued. 'And throw in plenty of nice yellow flowers as a treat for them. There's a good patch growing down by the tarn.'

I wheeled the barrow down to the tarn. Woundale's wild, golden daffodils might have finished flowering now – they bloom in spring – but the dandelions beside the tarn blazed like thousands of mini sunflowers. It was a beautiful sight. But how could I enjoy it today with a German airman lying in our favourite den?

When I'd filled the barrow, I took it to the mams' field and upended my load. I filled a second and had nearly done a third barrowload when I noticed Silent Simon watching me from further along the shore.

'What is it, Simon?' I called, going over to him.

He pointed at the woods and bared his teeth. For a moment I didn't know what he meant. Then, the penny dropped: 'Do you mean the Giant's Teeth?'

He nodded, and stuck his tongue out, like Sally did when she wanted to make you laugh. And I couldn't help but laugh now. Simon grinned too. I understood: 'Has Sally sent you?' I asked. Silent Simon nodded. 'Does she want to meet me at the Giant's Teeth?'

He nodded again.

'Now, Simon?'

Silent Simon shook his head, then mimed eating.

'After tea?'

Silent Simon nodded, then lumbered away. As I watched him go, I heard Sally's words again — *He's a deep one. He might not say much, but he knows . . .*

But after tea — bread with butter and jam on a Sunday — it wasn't so easy getting away. Stan, Auntie Dolly's young man, had arrived on his bike.

'Have you caught him?' Auntie Gladys and Auntie Dolly asked him at the same time.

Stan shook his head. 'I'm afraid not, they're sending us all back here. They think he might be hiding in Woundale after all. We have to search everywhere again in the morning.'

Auntie Gladys and Auntie Dolly gasped. I only just managed to stop myself from calling out in dismay. This was the last thing we wanted — Scarcross back with his 'pals', scouring the dale again.

'Oh, for goodness' sake. Why don't you all go to Morecombe with your buckets and spades whilst you're at it?' Auntie Annie said. 'You're more likely to find a German sunbathing on the beach than hiding in Woundale.'

'And another thing, Miss Grisedale,' Stan went on. 'I'm to ask you if you can billet some of us in your farmhouse. The rest of the lads are on their way.'

'Oh yes,' said Auntie Dolly quickly, as she stroked her curls. 'We'll make you all comfortable.'

'How many of you are there?' Auntie Annie asked.

'Eight of us,' Stan replied. 'The rest are staying with Sergeant Scarcross. They're already there.'

'Sergeant Scarcross?' Auntie Gladys asked.

Auntie Annie nodded. 'Aye, he was a sergeant in the last war.'

'Them lads billeting with Sergeant Scarcross,' Stan explained, 'all fought together in the last war.'

My aunties made up 'shake-me-down' beds in the kitchen and parlour. I had to bring down armfuls of blankets, cushions and pillows. Then I had to cut a couple of lettuces for the men, and collect some freshly laid eggs. When at last I did try to sneak away, two of the Home Guard had been stationed outside our house. I had to see Sally. With the Home Guard back here, and Scarcross in charge of them all, we really did need a plan, a brilliant one. And we needed it now. But how could I meet her without being seen?

7

My chance to get away without being noticed came at last. 'Here, Tommy,' said Auntie Annie. 'Take these cups of tea to the men outside.'

I carried the cups and saucers out to the Home Guards stationed on the farmyard.

'Thanks, lad,' one of them said. 'We were clamming for a nice cuppa.'

As they put their rifles down and lit their cigarettes, I pretended to go and see Mavis the pig. Then, edging round the byre, I melted away into the evening shadows.

I was soon in the woods. It was still light, but I felt as nervy as if it were the middle of the night. My mind spun. We were supposed to have met after tea. What had Sally been doing since then? Was she with the airman now? What if Scarcross found the airman tomorrow, and realised we'd been hiding him? And — harbouring an enemy combatant was illegal. In fact, didn't that make us traitors?

If only I could tell Auntie Annie. But I'd promised Sally. I could never break a promise to her.

I was just passing under the old oak on the way to the Giant's Teeth when someone jumped down from its branches. I only just managed to dive out of the way.

'Areet, bonny lad,' Sally grinned, pulling me to my feet. 'Divvent look so scared. What's taken you so long?'

'What do you think you're doing?' I cried, pushing her away.

She grinned, 'Just trying to see what it's like if you have to cut yourself down from a tree. Only just got here myself. Scarcross went all radgie when he came back. Crazy. Wild. Just cos I took the cart this morning. He locked me in the byre. That's why I had to send Silent Simon to you.'

'So how did you get out?'

Sally winked. 'Ways and means, marra, ways and means. Smellysnake is always saying I'm wild as a weasel, well mebbees I turned meself into a one and crawled through a hole, bit him on the ankle and ran right under his foot.'

Despite everything, I couldn't help but smile.

'That's better!' she grinned back. 'Nee point being like a wet weekend. Now howay, the Alleyman gadgie needs us.'

'Have you heard about the Home Guard?'

'Course I have, Tommy man. I heard Sergeant Stinkcrow talking to his gang about it. But divvent worry, I've got this.'

Sally reached behind the tree and brought out a sack. There was a clinking sound.

'What's in there?' I asked.

'Borrowed something from Sourcross, didn't I?'

'What?'

'Some bottles.'

'Some bottles. Bottles of what?'

'Whisky.'

'Whisky?'

'What are you, Tommy man, a flippin' parrot? Divvent keep repeating everything I say. Emptied them first, washed them oot and filled them with water. There's a bit of scran in there for him an' all.'

'Where did you get it all from, Sally?'

'Ask nee questions, Tommy man, and I won't tell you nee lies.'

For a moment the words Scarcross had said ran through my mind: *Nothing more than a thief*. But if someone's kept hungry, how can they be a thief when they steal a loaf of bread? And Sally hadn't even taken it for herself.

There was something else I wanted to know: 'Why did you ask Auntie Annie what an Alleyman is?'

'Heard Starecross say it,' she replied.

'It might make her suspicious,' I reasoned. 'Especially the way you ran off like that.'

But Sally was already heading towards the Giant's Teeth with her sack of swag.

We soon reached the stone circle. Once again, my heart started wrestling in my chest. If last time it had felt like a rat caught in a sack, now I felt as though I had half a dozen rats in there — the ones that had run over my feet this morning, and all of them twisting and writhing and biting as they tried to get out. Even an injured man can fire a pistol.

Sally moved aside the front door, and began crawling down the tunnel. The bottles in the sack clinked loudly as she pushed it in front of her. He'd definitely hear us coming. What if he thought we were the Home Guard? He'd have his Luger aimed and ready. No soldier would miss from such close range and Sally would be hit first. She was already peering into the giant's parlour. *Run, run, run*, my whole body wanted to scream. But all I said was: 'Is he still there?'

'Yes,' came Sally's whisper.

'Is he alive?'

'Divvent know. Still lying doon.'

Coming into the den myself, I could see the long boots. I could see the legs of his coveralls too. The thigh pockets bulged even more than I remembered. Sally was wrong, he could easily be hiding a signalling device, a radio — and a Luger too. She was leaning over him.

'Fast asleep,' she said. 'He must be ever so tired.'

'Get back,' I urged. 'You're too close.'

'Hello, it's me again,' she whispered to the airman.

'You'll wake him.'

'I want to. Hello, Alleyman gadgie. I'm Sally. And this is Tom, me marra. I'm sorry for poking you when you were up in the tree. And it wasn't us what fired them shotguns. You can trust us. We want to help. We haven't told neebody aboot you being here. Look, we've brought water.' As Sally reached into the sack to bring out one of Mr Scarcross's whisky bottles, I looked past her and saw the airman's face for the first time.

He didn't look like an enemy. He looked helpless. He was pale as a barn owl hunting under the moon. The cut over his eye really was shaped like a sickle. Red and swollen, it was encrusted with dry blood. I crawled a little closer so I could get a better view.

Suddenly, the German opened his eyes. Immediately, his hand moved to one of his bulging pockets. I froze. For a moment, I thought he was going to bring out a Luger. But he was too weak, and the hand dropped limply to his side.

He looked at Sally first. Then slowly his gaze travelled to me. He looked, but he didn't seem to see us. He was shivering.

'Here,' murmured Sally. 'Have some water.'

The German airman stared at the bottle as Sally held it out. His lips were cracked and dry. Gently, Sally lifted his head so that he could drink.

He took a few sips but most of the water ran down his chin.

'Howay, Alleyman,' Sally said. 'Take a proper gobful. Open your mouth wider.'

He took a deeper sip. And then almost a gulp. I'd often fed lambs like this. The ones that couldn't feed for themselves. The ones rejected by their mams. It was strange to see a grown man drink in the same, helpless way.

'That's better, isn't it?' Sally coaxed.

But she'd tilted the bottle too much and he spluttered as water coursed down his chin. Carefully she lowered his head back down onto his parachute pillow. The German airman just lay there.

'Look at him shivering,' Sally said. 'But he's hot. I'll leave the water here for you, gadgie Alleyman. To cool you down. And here's a bit of scran.' Reaching into the sack, she brought out some bread, but the German airman just stared vacantly at her.

'Divvent you want to eat, Alleyman gadgie?' Sally asked.

Now, the German airman stared at me, still without seeming to see me.

'Mebbees you'll be hungry later,' Sally continued. 'We'll leave it here for you, with the water. There's a bit of cheese an' all. Look, I'm leaving it where you can reach it.'

The German airman looked at the cheese and then closed his eyes.

Sally leant in even closer.

'Let's go now,' I said.

'Whisht, Tommy, he's sleeping again.'

He really did seem to be sleeping. Each time his chest rose and fell, the eagle on his heart seemed to flap its wings. Eagle? It looked more like a vulture — a vulture that was soaring over the whole of the world. He moaned slightly as he slept.

'He needs a doctor,' Sally murmured.

We waited, but he didn't wake, so we crawled back down

the tunnel. This time we made sure to put the 'front door' branches over the entrance. Sally led the way back through the trees. We stopped at the tarn. 'He looks so sad and lonely,' she said. 'Like a cloud in that poem. Only he's got nee daffs to cheer him up.' Sally too looked so sad and lonely that I could never have expected what she did next. Clapping her hands together, she burst into laughter. 'I've got it!' she cried.

'Got what?'

'Next bit of the plan.'

'It's too late for plans,' I said. 'We're just going to have to tell Auntie Annie.'

'No.' Sally shook her head. 'That's exactly what we cannet dee.'

'You said yourself he needs medical attention. What's the point in saving him from Scarcross if he just dies anyway?'

'He won't die.' Sally spoke quietly, but each word was heavy as a stone. 'Because we'll save him.'

'How, Sally, how?'

Once again, her laughter flew out over the tarn. 'How-how-how! Milk-a-dog-and-walk-a-cow. Find out tomorrow, won't you?'

'Tomorrow's a school day.'

'Exactly,' she shot back. 'Now howay, bonny lad, I'll walk you home. Can we gan through the hayfield?'

Before I could reply, she'd melted away into the dusk. There was nothing I could do but follow.

The cuckoo called from the willows. Vaulting a drystone

wall, we jumped down into the hayfield. The hayfield had to be untouched until late July, when it would be cut for winter hay. We weren't really supposed to walk in it until then, but Sally loved the wild flowers so much that I thought Auntie Annie wouldn't mind if we were careful not to crush the grass too much. I'd taught Sally the names of the flowers, and as we passed through them now, she tested herself. 'Betony,' she announced, paddling through the drifts of purple. 'And the blue eyes peeping up at us are milkwort. See them fluffy pink paws, Tommy? They're hare's-foot clover.'

'You're right.'

'Knew I was.'

As we waded on through the meadow, moths rose and danced in the air all around us. There were nightjars too, those strange birds of twilight. Chirring musically, they flitted over the meadow.

'No wonder that German gadgie came here,' Sally said. 'This is the most beautiful place in the whole world.'

Halfway across the hayfield, we were engulfed in a sweet, honey-like scent. Sally looked at me in wonder. 'What's that lovely smell, Tom?'

'Lady's bedstraw,' I explained, pointing at the froth of yellow flowers that could just be seen in the dying rays of the long summer's day.

'Why's it called that?'

I shrugged. 'I think in the olden days people used to put it in their mattresses.'

'With the feathers?'

'No, when everyone slept on straw.'

'Did everyone used to sleep on straw?' Sally asked.

'I think so. And they put these flowers in their beds so as to keep everything smelling nice. Auntie Annie still puts some in her drawer every summer.'

Kneeling down, Sally breathed in the honey fragrance. 'Lady's bedstraw,' she whispered.

She was still kneeling amongst the flowers when the barn owl appeared. Flapping slowly towards us, it seemed to float on its silent wings. Nearer and nearer it came, only seeming to see us at the last moment, when it suddenly lifted. For a few moments, it hovered directly above, and it seemed as though the airman was hanging there, gazing at us. Then the barn owl ghosted away over the meadow.

'I'll see you tomorrow,' Sally said, standing. 'And thanks.'

'What for?'

'Helping me save the German gadgie from Stinkcrab. You'll see tomorrow that it'll be all right. Honest it will. Have I ever lied to you?'

'No.'

The guards on our yard didn't even notice me sneak back in. One of them was leaning against the gate, dozing. The other was Stan. He was so busy chatting to Auntie Dolly, that he wouldn't have seen me pass even if I'd been on stilts and banging a drum.

I went into the house. Auntie Annie and Auntie Gladys

were sitting around the table with the rest of the good members of the Home Guard. The postman was with them. The room was littered with teapots, cups, saucers, cigarette smoke and gossip. There hadn't been such a gathering in the farmhouse for a long time. It was easy to slip through them unnoticed, and creep upstairs to bed.

TETHERA ...

1

The next morning, I woke to the sound of the kettle singing on the hob, and the Home Guard chatting in the kitchen. My aunties were making them breakfast. It was the first time I'd heard a man's voice down there at breakfast since my dad had left.

'Glad we could stay with you, Miss Grisedale,' one of the Home Guard was saying to Auntie Annie. 'I wouldn't fancy breakfast at Sergeant Scarcross's house.'

'You'd be lucky to get any,' another one laughed.

Connie jumped on my bed, licked me once, then raced back downstairs. She liked having the good members of the Home Guard around too.

'I've hoed the tatties for you,' Stan whispered to me when I came downstairs. 'Can't have you being late for school. And some of the other lads have started the milking.'

'Thanks, Stan,' I grinned.

After breakfast, I put on my satchel, got my bike from our byre and set off round the tarn to meet Sally as usual. The cuckoo was calling from the hayfield. Suddenly Sally came running towards me, her satchel banging against her side.

'Scram, Thomas!' she grinned, without stopping. 'Scram as fast as you can.'

Scarcross was chasing her. His angry shouts rang out over the water. I pedalled after her up the steeply rising road. 'Tried to stop us gannin' to school, didn't he?' Sally explained breathlessly. 'Told us I had to stay and clear stones from the bottom field.'

Scarcross had soon given up the chase. He stood in the dale below, shaking his fist. Throwing her head back, Sally tried to do her special 'who cares?' walk, but that's difficult to do when you're slogging uphill with a satchel over your shoulder. Then she started imitating Scarcross rubbing grease through his hair — with grunting pig noises to go with it. We both laughed so hard we could barely breathe.

It might be hard work pushing a bike out of Woundale up onto the fells, but once you reach the top, you can coast the rest of the way to town. And with Sally on the seat and me standing on the pedals in front of her, we were soon rolling as fast as a galloping horse.

Closing my eyes, I felt the wind ruffling my face and hair. Freewheeling down the long road, all our troubles seemed to be blown away.

'It's like the poem,' Sally shouted. 'We're a pair of clouds flying through the sky.'

The best bit of the whole journey was always the humpback

bridge over the beck. Even before we reached it, we both began to chuckle. We knew what was coming. Pedalling harder and harder, we sped up the sharp slope, then ramped off the top of the hump. And for an instant, we actually did fly. And our laughter flew with us.

After the bridge, I skidded to a halt and we both got off the bike. 'So what's the plan, Sal?'

'You ever lifted owt before, Tom?'

'Lifted?' I replied.

'Lifted,' Sally repeated. 'Borrowed something withoot the owner's consent.'

'Do you mean steal?'

'I mean lifted,' she repeated.

'As in, shoplifted?'

'I'm not talking aboot nee shops,' she said.

'No,' I returned. 'I've never lifted anything.'

She looked at me in amazement. 'Not ever?'

'Course not.'

'What, not ever took a single thing?' Sally asked, flabbergasted. I shook my head. 'Not even an apple or a farthing lying on the kerb?'

I felt as though I'd swallowed a large pebble. 'Is that the plan, Sally — stealing something. Don't you think we're in enough trouble without becoming thieves?'

'Divvent look at us like that, Thomas Grisedale,' she snapped. 'Sometimes things happen that leave you nee choice. Think you're better than me, divvent you? Well,

I'll dee it meself then, withoot your help. Cos I divvent need nee help me. Never have. Never will.' At that moment, I realised that Sally wasn't angry. She was sad. As though I'd been the only person in the world to understand her, and now even I didn't trust her. But I simply didn't know what to say. And neither did she. So we just got back on the bike.

By the time the town came into view, we still hadn't spoken. We freewheeled towards school, which was right beside the churchyard. The soldier was still guarding the wreckage.

As I put the bike in the bike shed, a gust of laughter came from the playground. Surrounded by a gaggle of smaller boys and girls, Bertie Tupperman was standing by the wall. They'd all been looking at the plane wreckage, but now everyone in the school was staring at Sally, and sniggering. Bertie Tupperman had obviously just called her a nasty name.

I waited for Sally to shout something back at him, but she didn't even seem to hear him. Instead, she just stood staring at the plane.

I could hear Bertie Tupperman chanting: 'Stinky-stinky-Geordie lass . . .'

'I want to help you,' I said. 'But I can't steal anything. It's wrong.'

'No one's stealing anything,' Sally said.

Unchecked by Sally, Bertie Tupperman's chanting grew louder. Even the other evacuees were joining in — they were too frightened not to. 'Pongy-pongy-Geordie lass, What she have for breakfast, A plate of grass . . .'

And all at once what Auntie Annie had said about Sally came back to me, how she was all alone in the world.

'Course I'll help you, Sally,' I said.

'Divvent put yourself oot, farm boy,' she replied. Then she smiled. 'Champion. This is the plan then. For the rest of the day, stay away from me. Nee matter what happens, keep your distance.'

'Why?'

'Just dee it, Tommy.'

'But I don't understand.'

'What's there to understand, man? All you have to dee is pretend you divvent know us. Tell everyone we've fallen oot, if you want. Just divvent try and help us, even if you think you should.'

'What if Bertie Tupperman starts on you?'

Sally's eyes sparked. 'He has to. Won't work withoot him. But I can't have you stopping him. You divvent know your own strength. You might be smaller than him but I bet you could lay Squirtyman oot with one right hook, I've seen the way you chop firewood. And that would ruin everything.'

'What's any of this got to do with the airman?' I demanded.

'Everything,' Sally returned.

I sighed. I knew Sally well enough to realise that she wasn't going to tell me anything more until she was ready. I was just going to have to trust her.

The chanting grew ever louder 'Geordie-Geordie-Geordie lass, Throw her in the dustbin, Chuck her out the class . . .'

Sally smiled. 'Are you ready, Tommy?'

The school bell began clanging. Miss Gently had come out onto the yard and was ringing it. The chanting stopped. Everybody lined up to go into school — a grey stone building, with a slate roof and small windows that always seemed to be watching you, like beady eyes. As the girls stood outside their entrance, the boys trooped over to their own door on the far side. Bertie Tupperman headed straight for Sally.

Instead of stopping him with a look, as she often did, she let him push her away. She staggered across the playground.

'Evacuee girl, Sally Smith, stop dawdling,' Miss Gently called. 'Didn't you hear the bell?'

'What was that, miss?' grinned Sally, as she slipped into school.

I hurried through the boys' entrance and hung up my jacket and satchel on a peg. There were only two classes in the school, infants (known as the babies) and juniors. I went into the junior class. Sally was already there.

'Good morning, juniors,' Miss Gently announced.

'Good morn-ing, Miss Gent-ly,' we piped back, each of us standing behind our desk.

'One two is two,' Miss Gently began.

'Two twos are four,' we chorused in return. 'Three twos are six, four twos are eight . . .'

Miss Gently always began the day like this. Beating time

with her long ruler, she hurried through the times tables, all the while watching us like an auctioneer watching farmers at a cattle sale. We all knew what she was looking for — a mistake.

The first slip-up was spotted in the six times table: 'Seven sixes are . . .'

The long ruler came crashing down on the desk and we all stopped dead. The ruler lifted from the desk and picked out a girl, whose long hair was so blond it was almost white.

'Emily Rebanks,' Miss Gently said. 'Go to the dunce's chair.'

Emily Rebanks was the shepherd's daughter. She was the youngest in our class. Head hanging, she went into the corner to sit on the high stool. Whoever made the first mistake had to sit there beside the draughty window. It wasn't so bad in summer, but in winter it was freezing. Emily Rebanks was usually the first to make a mistake. Not because she wasn't clever, as a shepherd's daughter she knew how to count better than anyone (you have to when you're working with sheep), but she was one of the pupils that Miss Gently really disliked. By staring directly at her, Miss Gently was usually able to fluster Emily into making a mistake. She tried it with Sally too, but it never worked.

'Begin sixes again,' Miss Gently commanded.

'One six is six,' we chanted. "Two sixes are twelve . . .'

Now the ruler started beating time more quickly. Like musicians following a crazy conductor, we all quickened.

The mistakes came thick and fast, each one greeted by a resounding smash of the ruler, which then pointed at the miscreant, who sat down. There was nothing Miss Gently liked so much as seeing us get things wrong.

I nearly made it to the end, but found the ruler pointing at me on eleven times eleven. I often get that one wrong.

Faster and faster went the ruler. By the end, Sally was the only one left standing, and we were all watching her. With a proud toss of her head, she sat down in her place on the back row. I sat in the middle of the class. Bertie Tupperman always sat in the seat closest to Miss Gently — and to the stove. Even if he was the first to make a mistake, he never had to sit on the dunce's stool. His dad was the butcher, and he always gave Miss Gently two pork sausages on a Friday afternoon. Bertie Tupperman was one of the few pupils Miss Gently liked. But how did he fit into Sally's plan? I was about to find out.

2

The chalk screeched as Miss Gently wrote sums on the blackboard. 'Most of you will get these wrong,' she gloated.

Her writing was so small that the numbers crowded each other like flies on a cowpat. Even if you were sitting near the front, you had to strain your eyes to see them. Emily Rebanks always got the sums wrong, because she couldn't see them properly from the dunce's corner.

Taking out our slates and chalk, we began to work. Miss Gently stalked around the class looking for mistakes, like a crow searching for a sickly lamb.

Looking up from my slate for a moment, I saw a piece of chalk fly over the class and strike Bertie Tupperman on the back of his head. Bertie Tupperman didn't react. He never put a foot wrong in Miss Gently's class. I looked back at Sally. She was busily working. But I knew she was the one who'd thrown the missile. Not long later, another piece of chalk struck Bertie Tupperman's neck. Sally winked at me. Bertie Tupperman still didn't look round.

'What's going on?' I asked her as the class began to file outside for playtime.

'Tupperman's not playing ball,' she said. 'That's what's gannin' on. But I'll make him. I'll catch him hook, line and sinker.'

'You sure you know what you're doing?' I asked.

'No, but once I get him outside, it's going to be a canny good laugh. Just wait and see.'

We were halfway to the door when Miss Gently called over: 'Not you, evacuee girl. You've got to practise your twelve times tables with Emily Rebanks.'

'That's not fair,' said Sally.

'Life isn't fair,' said Miss Gently. 'I would have thought you of all people would know that by now.' Miss Gently turned to me. 'Out you go then, Thomas Grisedale.'

After playtime, Miss Gently went to the infants and Miss Jameson came to us.

'Hello, children,' Miss Jameson greeted us. It was as though someone had opened the windows and let fresh air in. 'Who would like to do some singing?'

We all put our hands up. Everybody liked Miss Jameson.

'Emily, would you bring out the radiogram, please?' Miss Jameson asked. 'And Sally would you give her a hand?'

Sally and Emily wheeled the radiogram over from the cupboard. With its built-in loudspeaker and dials, the radiogram was massive — about the size of our pig Mavis.

'Turn the radiogram on, please, Emily,' Miss Jameson

instructed. 'And can you and Sally hand out the singing books too.'

Miss Jameson always got Emily to help her, I think it was her way of getting her off the dunce's stool. She usually asked one of the evacuees to help as well.

The radiogram glowed into life. The programme was just starting: 'Hello children,' said the presenter.

'Hello, radiogram,' we all called back.

'Welcome to *Singing Together*,' the presenter announced. 'Are you all healthy and happy today and ready for some singing?'

'Yes, thank you,' we all called back.

It really did feel as though there was a person inside that huge wooden box talking to us. And an orchestra too — for soon the first song began. As we all sang along, I could hear Sally whistling through her teeth. 'Proper Geordie song,' she grinned:

'Bobby Shafto's gone to sea,
Silver buckles at his knee,
He'll come back and marry me,
Bonny Bobby Shafto . . .'

After this, we sang 'D'ye ken John Peel?' Then: 'Donkey Riding, Cockles and Mussels'. And so on, until the dinner bell was ringing.

'Thank you,' said Miss Jameson. 'It's been like listening to angels.'

The 'babies' ate their dinner first. We 'big ones' went out onto the playground to wait for them to finish. On the yard we could always smell our dinner. It was the same every Monday: squelchy cabbage, rock hard beetroot and rubbery spam. But we ate every bite — you had to. Something else was the same today as well. Now that no teachers were around, Bertie Tupperman was trying to annoy Sally. But something was different — she didn't say anything to shut him up. What on earth was she up to?

Bertie Tupperman started clapping his hands and chanting softly: 'Sally-Smith's, Mam's a witch, She left her in a Tyneside ditch.'

I waited for Sally to stop him, but she didn't. Instead, she picked up a stone and started playing hopscotch. Keeping out of the way as I had promised, I leant against the wall, and watched.

The clapping and chanting grew louder. The others joined in, until the mocking words roared like a fire. Meanwhile, Sally calmly hopped her way up the chalked markings of the hopscotch court.

Followed by the rest of the class, Bertie Tupperman got closer and closer to her. Still no reaction. He couldn't believe his luck. Suddenly, he held his hand up, and the clapping and chanting stopped. In the silence, I heard Bertie Tupperman spit. His heavy gob flew through the air, breaking at Sally's feet, like a rotten egg. She'd just hopped onto number seven.

As Sally bent down to pick up the stone, Bertie Tupperman snatched it from her.

'Is it true what they say about Tyneside,' he said, 'that you all eat dog cack sandwiches?'

I saw Sally's eyes glint like the sun on a sickle blade. But she still didn't react. I had to stop myself from going over.

'You smell,' Bertie Tupperman said, holding his nose. 'No wonder your mam and dad don't want you.'

He threw the stone over the wall towards the wrecked plane. Still Sally didn't react. Cock-a-hoop, Bertie Tupperman reached out to give her one of his 'horse bites' — a savage nip to your arm, made even worse by his long, filthy fingernails — but before he could, Sally darted in at him to whisper something in his ear. Suddenly he screamed, and clutching the side of his head, dropped to the ground.

3

Sally stood over the bully. In stunned silence, the whole class gathered round. All you could hear was Bertie Tupperman squealing as he held his ear. It sounded as loud as when the bomber flew low over Woundale.

'Sally Smith, evacuee girl,' a voice called out.

Miss Gently was striding over.

'Sally Smith!' she roared.

'That's me name,' Sally replied calmly. 'Divvent wear it oot.'

'You dirty beast,' Miss Gently hissed. 'I saw what you did. You bit that boy's ear. You filthy, Tyneside animal.'

Miss Gently reached out to grab her, but Sally shrugged her off so powerfully that the teacher was sent staggering away. Everyone gasped.

Sally walked over to her. 'Sticks and stones may break my bones,' she said, 'but names can never hurt me.'

Miss Gently stepped back as Sally headed to the school. The watching crowd parted for her like the Red Sea we'd heard about in chapel on Sunday. Head up, arms swinging

and feet kicking high, Sally marched towards the boys'
entrance.

'Sally Smith!' Miss Gently yelled. 'Don't you dare go
through the boys' entrance.'

With a wide grin, Sally continued into school, straight
through the boys' entrance.

Sally was sent to stand outside the staffroom. The rest of
us had Miss Gently again all afternoon. She gave us one
spelling test after another. It was nearly home time when
there was a knock at the classroom door.

It was Miss Jameson. 'Excuse me, Miss Gently, can I have
your assistance for a moment?'

The class was left alone but there was no trouble: Bertie
Tupperman had gone home.

'Tommy, tell her thank you,' Emily Rebanks suddenly
said. 'Tell Sally, I'm glad she bit him.'

'So am I,' someone else said.

'And me,' whispered a third.

'We all are,' a fourth one said.

The rest of the class nodded. Then the door was flung
back open.

'All girls come with me now,' commanded Miss Gently,
her face puce.

Without a word, the girls filed out of the classroom after her.

'You boys as well, please,' Miss Jameson told us quietly.

We all trooped after Miss Jameson to the cloakroom. Sally
was there.

'Children,' Miss Gently announced. 'We have a thief in our midst. Every girl, stand beside your peg. Miss Jameson and I are going to come round and look in your satchels. You too,' she growled at Sally.

Sally walked to her peg.

'Boys as well, please,' said Miss Jameson. 'Stand in front of your peg.'

'Hurry up,' Miss Gently snapped. The pegs were arranged alphabetically. 'Right, Doris Armstrong, open your satchel.' Doris Armstrong did, but Miss Gently hardly looked inside. Instead, she was glaring at Sally. She quickly moved down the alphabet line, barely looking in each satchel but always scowling at Sally.

Irene Atkinson ... Nancy Bell ... Florence Blennerhassett ...

'Don't you think we should search them properly?' Miss Jameson whispered, but we could still hear her.

'Don't be stupid,' Miss Gently hissed, making no attempt to keep her voice down. 'I know exactly who the culprit is.'

'It's more likely someone's broken in from outside,' said Miss Jameson. 'Maybe it was that German navigator everyone's talking about. They still haven't found him.'

'I'm telling you, it's Sally Smith,' Miss Gently snapped. 'She's been standing outside the staffroom all afternoon.'

Freda Easton ... Dorothy Hancock ... Muriel Hewlett ...

I looked at Sally. Her face was blank.

Elsie Kettleworth ... Martha Postlethwaite ...

Still, no sign of reaction from Sally.

Emily Rebanks ... Joyce Robson ... Eileen Shields ...

At last, 'Sally Smith!' declared Miss Gently, thrusting her hand triumphantly into Sally's satchel.

But whatever she was looking for wasn't there. Miss Gently brought out the exercise book and pencil that Auntie Annie had given Sally. Miss Gently croaked in disbelief. 'Where is it?' she demanded.

'Where's what, Miss Gently?' Sally replied innocently.

'You know, girl!' Grabbing hold of Sally, Miss Gently began to shake her. 'Where is it?' she shouted. 'Where have you put it?'

'That's enough, Miss Gently,' said Miss Jameson.

But the shaking was growing more and more wild, until Sally's head bounced about as though she were Tilly, her rag doll.

'I said that's enough, Miss Gently,' said Miss Jameson, and with a force that you wouldn't have expected, she slapped Miss Gently across her face.

The shaking stopped instantly. Miss Gently ran from the changing room, and slammed the staffroom door behind her.

'Right, children,' Miss Jameson said, taking a deep breath. 'It seems that someone has broken into the staffroom and stolen something very valuable. Miss Gently made a mistake. She thought one of us was the thief. But no one here is a thief. Now, everyone please get your satchels and go home. And, Sally, I'm very sorry about Miss Gently's mistake.'

I was reaching up for my own satchel when I realised that it was heavier than usual. The leather bulged. Something big and heavy had been stuffed inside.

4

With Sally sitting on the saddle and the heavy satchel over my shoulder, I pedalled out of town as quickly as I could. The moment the houses and church had fallen from view, I braked sharply.

'What you deein'?' Sally demanded.

'Seeing what's in here,' I snapped, jabbing my finger at the satchel.

Sally looked back the way we'd come. 'Are you off your chump, Tommy man? You divvent nosh the apples till you're well oot of the orchard.'

'What's that supposed to mean?'

'It means, keep pedalling, and divvent stop until I say.'

Standing up on the pedals, I carried on. I was so furious I couldn't speak.

'I knew they wouldn't search you,' Sally said.

'What if they had?' I shot back.

'I'd have said I put it there. Honest I would. Divvent gan all moody, Thomas. It's not as if I've nicked it for meself.'

'Nicked what?'

Sally's answer was an infuriating giggle. 'Find oot soon, won't you?'

At last we reached the humpback bridge. I'd never been so angry with Sally.

'Howay,' grinned Sally. 'Now I'll show you.'

We got off the bike.

'Under here first,' called Sally as she ran down beneath the bridge. 'In case anybody comes.'

Leaning my bike against the stonework, I joined her. It was like a cave under the bridge. The beck ran by at our feet. A thick clump of alders grew at the far end, blocking us in.

'Open it then, Tommy man,' Sally said, her excited voice echoing under the arch.

I unbuckled the satchel and brought out a large, battered, black tin. On the lid was a red cross and the words: *Emergency use only.*

'Took it from the staffroom, didn't I?' Sally whispered.

'You've stolen the school first aid kit?' I asked in disbelief.

'What else was I supposed to do, Tommy man? You saw the gash on the Alleyman's head. You said yourself we cannet just let him die.'

The lid was stiff. When I'd managed to prise it off, a sharp, astringent smell rose up. The tin was stuffed with medical supplies. I reached in to take a bandage wrapped in paper, but Sally stopped me.

'That's medical equipment,' she said. 'Not a toy.'

And snatching the lid, she put it firmly back on.

'Tell you what, mind,' she said. 'Dirty Rubberman's ear could have done with some medical attention.'

Then she grabbed her ear and squealed, and I couldn't help but burst into laughter. Neither could she. Sally could make me smile even on the saddest of days. She made me laugh — even in the middle of a war.

'Did you really plan to bite him?' I asked.

She shook her head. 'I'm not proud of it, but when I saw his stupid face pushing so near me, I couldn't stop meself. It wasn't much. Just a little nip.'

'And that was your master plan — get put outside the staffroom all afternoon so you could nick this?'

'Wasn't just that. You see I didn't want to have stand there all day and miss me dinner. And the cook's in and out of the staffroom all morning. But most of all, I just wanted to give Bully Bertie a taste of his own medicine at the same time. And it worked. Howay, let's get this to the airman.'

We were climbing back on the bike when I suddenly remembered how we'd left Woundale that morning: 'What about Scarcross?'

'I'm not bothered about him.'

'And the Home Guard will have been searching Woundale all day. They might have found the airman, Sal.'

'No, they won't. So long as you shut the front door, that den's the best hiding place in all of England.'

'But they'll be everywhere.'

'Nothing and nobody will stop us getting this to our

Alleyman gadgie,' Sally returned. 'Even if Hitler and the whole bloomin' German army set up a roadblock, me and you are going to find a way past. We're on a mission. Now pedal as fast as you can, Tommy man.'

I shook my head. 'Get off the bike,' I said. 'I've got a better idea.'

I wheeled the bike under the bridge, so that it was hidden from the road above.

'We'll use the back door,' I decided.

'Back door?'

'The secret way into Woundale.'

'There's a secret way?' Sally asked.

'And if we go that way, neither Scarcross nor the Home Guard will know we're back in the valley.'

Sally's eyes widened. 'You've never said anything aboot a secret way.'

I shrugged. 'We've never needed it before. I'll leave the bike here under the bridge and get it on the way to school tomorrow. Now, come on.'

Abandoning the bike and the road, we followed the beck downstream as it ran over the fell. The current grew quicker and quicker as we approached Woundale.

Sally clutched at my arm: 'We're gannin' to the force, aren't we?'

The force, that wide curtain of water, which tumbles down from the fells into Woundale.

I nodded.

'Isn't it proper dangerous?'

I nodded again. 'But it's the only way of getting to him without being seen.'

We heard the force before we saw it: a roar that grew louder and louder. Then we smelt it — the zesty tang of tumbling water.

'Slow down,' I warned Sally, who was hurrying ahead. 'You'll have to follow me. You don't know the safe way down.'

She crossed her eyes, but let me lead the way through the rowans growing thickly on the bank of the beck. Then we stepped out of the trees and found that the land had suddenly stopped. Bubbling and churning, the beck hurled itself over the drop: a precipice even higher than our house. For a few moments we just stood there.

'There's a secret path,' I called over the roar of the cascading water. 'If you know where to look. My dad showed me, just before he left.'

'Why?' Sally asked.

'Why what?'

'Why did he only show you when he left?'

'I don't know,' I said. 'Maybe in case there's an invasion and we need to escape.'

But standing there now, I wondered if there was another reason he'd told me about it as he was leaving— in case he never came back and didn't have another chance.

'It's the back door into Woundale,' I said. 'But you have to be so careful. If your foot slips . . .'

5

'You come down after me,' I shouted. 'Keep tight hold of your satchel. Do everything I do.'

'Even if you pick your nose?' Sally returned, but when I looked round at her, I could tell that she was concentrating hard.

It wasn't really a path, more a flight of stairs worn into the rock — a flight of very slippery, uneven stairs. Birch trees grew out of the stone.

'Give me a drainpipe any day,' Sally said.

'Use the trees to steady yourself,' I shouted, trying to sound braver than I felt. 'Like bannisters on stairs.'

Taking a deep breath, I stretched out my foot and began to descend. Just as Dad had shown me, I grabbed the first birch. But I hadn't been carrying a cumbersome satchel when he'd guided me down. I clung to the trunk until I felt secure enough to lower myself to the next tree.

'I've seen faster snails crawling up Scarcross's kitchen wall,' Sally called.

'The stairs get wider apart, the further you go,' I yelled.

Both of us fell silent as we concentrated on the descent. The 'stairs' did get wider apart, and I was soon sweating. At the same time though, I felt a lovely cooling sensation — it was the fine spray rising from the white water. The lower I got, the spray grew cooler, and the roar of water, louder.

When I looked up, I saw that Sally was coming down just as carefully.

Suddenly, the 'stairs' stopped.

'First throw your satchel down. Aim for the sand,' I hollered, and taking my satchel off, let it drop.

'Now you do this,' I shouted, and making sure she was watching, grabbed hold of a branch on the last tree, and dangled myself down. Closing my eyes, I let myself go.

Then I was landing in the sand right by the plunge pool. Jumping up, I grabbed the heavy satchel and moved out the way. On the rock above, Sally was working her way down. I watched her reach the last tree. Then, just as I had told her, she threw down her satchel. She closed her eyes too, but instead of dropping, she clung on tightly.

'Just jump,' I said.

She didn't stick her tongue out at me. She didn't pull a funny face. She didn't move.

'The sand's soft,' I encouraged her.

'But what if I land in the water?' she called down, eyes still tight shut.

'You won't,' I said. 'Just jump where I did.'

'But if I dee?'

For the first time since I'd known her, Sally seemed to be frightened.

'I cannet swim,' she said.

'I can,' I returned. 'I'll pull you out if you fall in.'

For a few more moments she didn't move then suddenly she opened her eyes, threw her head back, and with a loud 'weehee', let herself drop. She landed in the sand and jumped straight up with a huge grin. 'Divvent need nee help, me,' she said. 'Never have. Never will.'

Suddenly, her eyes filled with wonder.

'Look,' she gasped.

I followed her pointing finger to the force.

'A rainbow,' she said.

A rainbow was arcing through the force. This happened sometimes. There had been a rainbow in the force on the day my dad and I had climbed down too.

'A rainbow,' she repeated. 'Doesn't that mean everything's going to be all right?'

I was going to explain to Sally that a rainbow was made by the sun shining on the fine droplets of water. But instead I heard myself say: 'Yes, it means everything's going to be all right.'

And I could see that Sally believed me. If only I could believe it as well.

We were soon working our way through the woods that covered that whole steep side of Woundale. We got so near to our farmhouse that we could even smell Mavis the pig.

Questions buzzed in my mind like wasps round a jam sandwich. What if Scarcross had already found him and his empty whisky bottles — and knew we'd helped him. What if the German airman had recovered? What if he really was part of an invasion and he was waiting to spring out and take us prisoner? I tried to swat these thoughts away, but they kept buzzing in my head.

There was no sign of Scarcross nor the Home Guard. We soon reached the Giant's Teeth. The front door was safely in place. I hardly noticed the thorns as I followed Sally down the tunnel.

'Divvent worry, German gadgie,' Sally called. 'It's just me and Tommy.'

When we got into the den the German airman was still lying down, but he was wide awake. And his hand was in his pocket. The blood rushed in my ears like the force. I tried to warn Sally about the Luger but I couldn't speak.

Eyes darting, the airman stared down the tunnel past us. When he saw that we were alone, he brought his hand out of his pocket.

'Told you we'd come back, didn't I?' Sally said. 'I'm ever so glad you've eaten all your scran and drunk your water.' She pointed at the empty bottles. 'But that wound of yours is worse. And you're still all shivery and hot.'

I looked at the gash on his head. It was swollen and raw. Yellow pus was oozing out, like the fatty guts of a chicken.

'Just as well we've brought you something to make you

better,' Sally went on. 'Tommy's got it. Haven't you, Tommy? Howay, man, open the satchel.'

I unfastened the buckle of the satchel and pulled out the first aid kit. Sally took off the lid and offered the kit to the airman. He stared at it, but didn't move. 'Howay, Mr Alleyman,' Sally said. 'This will make you better.'

He seemed to understand. Lifting himself by his elbows, he managed to sit up. Then he reached out.

'Look out, Sally,' I whispered.

'He only wants a dressing for his wound, Tommy man,' she said.

She handed him a bandage. The airman took it. But then sank back down.

'He's still weak and dopey,' Sally said. 'I'll have to help him.'

'But you don't know what to do,' I said.

'What's that supposed to mean?' she demanded.

'I mean, you're not a nurse are you?'

'Oh aye, and you're the world-famous Doctor Dolittle, are you?'

'Course not.'

'Well, one of us has to dee it. Howay, we can swap places if you want.'

'I'm not saying that.'

'Then what are you saying, Tommy man?'

At that moment, the German airman's boot knocked my knee. The sudden touch jolted me like a rat bite. He was trying to shuffle closer to us. The effort made him groan.

Suddenly, Sally gasped. 'Look,' she whispered, pointing at his mouth. 'Can you see?'

'Move further back,' I urged.

'Look at his teeth, Tommy.'

When the airman groaned again, mouth wide, I could see what she meant.

'He's got a lucky gap,' she said. 'Just like me.'

The German airman did indeed have a gap between his two front teeth. At that moment he began coughing. His whole body shook with the loud hacking.

'He needs the water now,' Sally decided.

'*Wasser*,' the airman nodded.

'That must mean water, Tommy. You want more *wasser*, Alleyman? We'll get you *wasser*. Plenty of the best *wasser* in the world.' She thrust the two empty whisky bottles at me. 'Howay, Tommy, gan and fill them.'

'What, and leave you here?'

'Why aye, man. I can look after meself.'

'But—'

'Just gan and dee it! Look at him, man, he's aboot as dangerous as a newborn lamb.'

'*Bring mir Wasser*,' the airman begged.

'Aye,' smiled Sally. 'We'll bring you *wasser*.' She grabbed my satchel and rooted about inside. 'This is for you an' all, Mr Alleyman.'

'What else have you put in there?' I asked, staring at the thick wedge of spam she brought out.

'Just this,' said Sally, lifting up a large hunk of bread and an apple.

'Did you get them from the school kitchen?'

'Ask nee questions and I'll tell nee lies,' she replied. 'Now howay, and bring him his *wasser*.'

Backing out of the tunnel with the bottles, I ran to where a little beck gurgled down the hillside, ice cold and sweet. It seemed to take forever for the bottles to fill. Looking out for Scarcross and the Home Guard, I ran back as fast as I could.

I was greeted by the reek of iodine, and the sight of the German airman lying flat on his back with his eyes closed. There was a bandage round his head.

'What have you got there, Sally?' I gasped.

She was holding a large knife. 'Take this,' she said, thrusting it at me.

I took it by the handle. It had a swastika on the top. The Nazi eagle was perched above the blade — it was a Luftwaffe dagger.

'Borrowed it from him, didn't I?' she explained. 'Needed to cut the bandage. I used these on his heed and knee.' She lifted up two small bottles. 'Stinks to high heaven an' all. I could tell it hurt him when I put it on, but he didn't squeal or anything.'

I couldn't move. All I could do was stare at the eagle on the knife. I stabbed it into the ground. The blade disappeared, but the eagle remained — and the swastika.

'Here's the *wasser*,' Sally whispered, holding a bottle to his cheek. 'Nice cold *wasser*.'

The German airman opened his eyes and tried to lift his bandaged head. But the effort of getting the bandage on seemed to have made him groggier than ever. Sally helped him lift his head. Then she raised the bottle to his mouth. Most of the water dribbled down his chin. When a sickly lamb drank like this, you knew that it wouldn't see out the night.

'*Danke*,' he murmured.

'That must mean thank you,' she whispered.

'*Danke*,' the airman repeated. Then, exhausted, he fell into a restless sleep. He moaned a few times.

'He's having a bad dream,' Sally murmured.

We watched him for a while.

'What now?' I asked.

'We scram,' Sally said. 'That's what. Visiting time at the Sally Smith Hospital is over — just got to let him get plenty of bed rest. And once he's scoffed the scran, he'll be right as rain.'

6

'Best get meself back,' Sally said as we came out of the woods. And she started walking towards the Scarcross place.

I followed.

Sally shook her head. 'Isn't it your teatime soon?'

'But Scarcross—'

'How many times have I got to tell you, Thomas Grisedale? Divvent need nee help, me.'

'Never have. Never will,' we both said together.

Sally laughed. 'I'll sort Scaresnake oot, divvent worry aboot that. If he tangles with me, he'll wish he hadn't. Now buzz off. It's Monday, you have your favourite tea on Mondays divvent you — bubble and squeak?'

When I got home Connie was waiting at the gate. I knelt down and let her lick me. Everyone else was too busy to notice that I was late back from school.

'Hello, love,' said Auntie Dolly, carrying a bucket of vegetable peelings over to Mavis's pigsty. 'Have you heard the news?'

I shook my head.

'The Home Guard have gone,' said Auntie Gladys from the door. 'Postman said that someone said that an old man over the far side of Cat Fell heard someone trying to raid his henhouse last night.'

'They've been ordered to search there,' said Auntie Dolly.

'Has Mr Scarcross gone with them?' I asked.

Auntie Gladys shook her head. 'He's gone with Mr Rebanks and his dogs to bring their sheep in from the fells.'

'Shearing tomorrow,' Auntie Dolly continued. 'Because the weather looks set fair. The Hawkrigg brothers are gathering their flock in now. Stan said they'll bring ours down as well this year.'

The Woundale sheep clipping was an annual event. All the fell farmers in the area brought their sheep down to our dale for it.

If Scarcross was gathering his sheep in, he might well be gone all night. Good news for Sally.

'Can you water the cows, Tommy?' Auntie Annie called from inside the house.

'Take Vi for a quick paddle when you do, Tommy,' Auntie Gladys put in.

I took Vi and the mams and their calves down to the tarn. Connie came too. As the cows drank, I stood my little cousin in the water and held her steady. The tarn lapped gently against us. The cuckoo called from the rushes and then from the willows. Everything was so calm. But trouble was brewing: Scarcross, Miss Gently, Bertie Tupperman's ear, the stolen first aid kit, not to mention the German airman.

Kicking the water, Vi suddenly laughed with delight. But I didn't. When a shining blue hawker dragonfly came dancing over the water, she pointed in wonder as it inspected us. We could hear its wings whirring. It was so blue that it was as though a few drops of the tarn had grown wings. But even this didn't interest me today.

'Did they drink plenty?' Auntie Annie asked as I came into the kitchen.

'Yes, Auntie Annie.'

'We'll maybe get a bit of extra milk tomorrow then.'

'And did Vi have a good kick?' Auntie Gladys asked.

'Laughed her head off,' I said.

'Wash your hands, and hang up your satchel, love,' said Auntie Annie. 'Tea's ready in a minute.'

It was only after I'd washed my hands and gone upstairs that I realised I'd made a mistake. Hanging the satchel on the hook behind my door, I saw I had Sally's satchel instead of my own.

'Tea's on the table,' Auntie Annie called from downstairs.

I hurried down to find a plate of bubble and squeak waiting for me. Made with the potato and cabbage leftovers from Sunday dinner, Auntie Annie always managed to turn it into one of the highlights of the week. But it's hard to enjoy your tea when you're hiding an enemy combatant.

'Had a good day at school, Tommy?' Auntie Annie asked.

I nodded.

'Sally all right?' Auntie Dolly asked.

I nodded again.

'So no one knows in town?' Auntie Gladys put in.

My stomach lurched. 'Knows what?' I replied.

'About the airman being heard at Cat Fell,' she added.

'No one mentioned it, Auntie Gladys.'

'Yet another wild goose chase,' remarked Auntie Annie.

I ate in silence.

'You're quiet today, Tommy,' Auntie Annie remarked.

Did Auntie Annie sense something was up? I was going to have to throw her off the scent before she began asking questions. I felt a lie rise onto my tongue. Before I could stop it, the lie was on my lips. 'Actually,' I heard myself say, 'people are saying that there might not have been a navigator on board at all. They reckon it was just a four-man crew.'

'There,' said Auntie Annie triumphantly. 'It's what I've said right from the start. Now we can stop all the tittle-tattle and get back to our farm work. Thomas, will you scythe the nettles after tea?'

After tea, as I went upstairs to get my thick gloves so I wouldn't get any nettle stings, Sally's satchel caught my eye. Hers was much cleaner than mine. The buckles glinted too. Before I realised what I was doing, I'd opened it.

Inside, I could see the exercise book and pencil. There was a handful of rags too — I pulled out Sally's rag doll.

This was the excuse I'd been looking for. Sally had said

she didn't want me to help her, but she always wanted her doll. I'd take Tilly over to her now and swap the satchels back. At the same time, I could help her with any jobs that needed doing, and check that Scarcross hadn't come back early.

I was pushing Tilly back into the satchel when my fingers brushed against something else. I drew it out. It was a piece of string — attached to some cardboard. I knew instantly what it was: an evacuee label. And Auntie Dolly had said that Sally arrived without one! Now I'd find out exactly where she was from.

Only I didn't. Sally's name wasn't written on the tag. Instead, there was a name I'd never heard before — *Ethel Kirkup, 18 Woodside Gardens, Dunston, County Durham.*

7

When Connie saw me coming onto the yard, she bounded over to the nettles. 'We'll scythe later,' I told her, holding up the satchel. 'We're going to see Sally first.'

Sally? Was she Sally Smith or was she Ethel Kirkup? I had always thought that whatever she said to others, she would tell me the truth. Had she been lying about herself all this time?

Connie and I ran round the tarn. Arnold neighed in greeting from his field. Whenever she could, Sally would take him outside to feel the sun on his back. Then we crept onto Scarcross's yard. Hiding behind the rusty plough, we both listened. Connie sniffed the air, then licked me. There was no immediate danger, Connie could always tell if there was. Scarcross must still be up on the fells gathering his flock. Connie headed for the byre. Sally was probably working in there.

I followed Connie and told her to stay outside. Someone needed to keep a look out.

The byre was dark. I couldn't see Sally anywhere; I couldn't hear her working either. A swallow darted in through a gap in the wall and flew up to its nest in the rafters. The sound of its nestlings chirping filled the byre. When the swallow had gone, I could only hear the mice scuttling through the shadows.

'Told you not to come,' a familiar voice came down from the hayloft.

'Is your name really Sally Smith?' I asked, not knowing what else to say.

There was a pause. 'Mebbees.'

'Or are you Ethel Kirkup?'

'I'm not her.'

'Well, who are you then?'

I waited for her to explain. But she didn't. I waited for her to speak, to say anything, but she didn't. Instead, she lowered the hayloft ladder, so I climbed up.

I was crawling through the open hatch, when a beam of light dazzled my eyes. Sally was sitting in the hay, pointing a torch at me.

'Do you like my new Eveready torch?' she asked. 'Borrowed it from old Snakecross.'

The torchlight gave her a strange look. For a moment it was as though she really were a different person to my friend Sally.

'How did you find oot?' she asked.

I opened her satchel and brought out the rag doll.

'What are you deein' with Tilly?' she demanded, snatching the doll.

'We got our satchels mixed up.'

'Hold on a minute,' Sally said. 'Let me check my wardrobe.'

She stood up, and shining the torch behind, reached up to one of the rafters and plucked down my satchel. Thrusting it at me, she snatched her own back.

But I was still staring in disbelief at what I'd just seen in the torch beam. As well as the satchel, a woollen cardigan had hung from the rafter and a pair of boots — both given to her by Auntie Annie. I could also see an old, dirty pillow and a blanket on the straw.

'Is this where you live?' I cried.

For a moment I could tell she was going to pretend to be Scarcross doing something stupid. But instead she smiled sadly. 'Why aye, welcome to me home sweet home.'

'You live in the byre?'

'Unless it's suddenly turned into a room at the Royal Station Hotel.'

'Why didn't you tell me?'

'I don't have to tell you everything.'

'Have you spent all winter up here?'

'For your information, I slept doonstairs when it was really cold. Me and Arnold kept each other company. He's canny warm, and when he lies doon he lets you snuggle right into him. Divvent look so worried, Tommy. It's not so bad, just as long as you make friends with all the mice and rats.'

But I couldn't laugh. Woundale had had lots of frosts and snow last winter.

'And I've got this now an' all,' she said, and reaching into the straw under the blanket, brought out a handful of sweet-smelling flowers.

'Lady's bedstraw,' I whispered.

'Went and picked meself some,' she nodded. 'Why aye, I've known far worse than this.'

'Known worse?' I asked in disbelief. 'Where?'

'Questions, questions, questions,' cried Sally. 'Who put you in charge of the world all of a sudden?'

'I thought we were friends,' I said. 'But I didn't even know that you've been living in a byre. Let alone what your real name is.'

'Neither do I,' she said quietly, hugging her doll close.

'What do you mean by that?'

'What I mean by that, Tommy man, is that I have nee idea what me proper name is either.'

'I don't understand.'

'Then understand this, Tommy Clotdale. Neebody ever told me what I'm called.'

'What about your mam and dad?'

Sally shrugged. 'Divvent kna who they are.'

'I'm sorry,' I stammered.

'Nee need to be sorry. If neeone gives you a name, it just means you get to choose one for yourself. One you like. And that's why I'm called Sally Smith.'

'You chose your own name?'

'Why aye, bonny lad. Sally Smith.'

'When?' I asked. 'How? Why?'

'Canny long story, that,' Sally replied. 'If I tell you, I'll have to tell you a lot more besides. Then you might even get to know why I divvent mind sleeping in a byre.' Though her voice was serious, in the light of the Eveready torch I saw a half-smile play on her face. 'Want to know, Tommy man?'

'Course I do.'

'We'll have to ask someone first,' she said. 'She'll decide whether we should share our secrets.' Sally pretended that Tilly was whispering in her ear. Then she nodded. 'Tilly says, Why aye, tell him. Tilly says, Tommy Grisedale's a bobby dazzler. Tilly says, Trust him.' Sally looked me right in the eye. 'Really want to know who I am, do you?'

'I do.'

'Well,' said Sally. 'I cannet tell you everything. Cos only Tilly knows the whole story.'

'What are you talking about, Sally?'

'The story of Sally Smith, from the beginning — that's what I'm talking aboot. Well not reet from the beginning. I divvent kna where the beginning starts. Tilly remembers more than me, but she isn't telling. What I can remember, starts with *wasser*.'

'*Wasser?*'

'Keep up, slowcoach. *Wasser* is water.' Sally took a deep breath. 'Once upon a time, they found a little lass paddling in a big river. They didn't know how she got there or where she was supposed to be gannin'. Had someone left her there? Was anyone waiting at home for her to come back? Neebody knew. All they knew was that the river was big and she was small. And that she had a rag doll in her arms. So they snatched her oot of the water before the poor mite would droon.'

'And that was you?'

'Well done, smartypants.'

'Who rescued you?' I asked.

Sally smiled. 'Old Auntie Jinny — and her cats. She wasn't me real auntie. Not like yours. But she took us in to live with her. She called us Sally Salmon. Cos she'd fished us oot of the river. Usually she rescued cats; I was the only stray girl she ever took in. Old Auntie Jinny tried to find oot who I was. Took us roond the hooses asking. Some wifie said they'd seen us playing at the Dunston Staiths. Another one said that I used to pet the pit ponies up at Watergate Colliery. Some gadgie swore doon I was the bargeman's daughter, cos they'd seen us on a coal barge. But neeone knew for sure. Then Old Jinny died.' Sally shone the Eveready torch up into the beams, and we watched a swallow dart into its nest, then fly out again. 'God bless her all the way to heaven,' she whispered.

'What happened to you then?'

'Hinny Carstairs took us in, didn't she? Why, she already had ten bairns, so one more didn't matter. They called us Sally Cats at Hinny Carstairs's hoose. What with me having come from Old Jinny's. I had to fight for me supper a bit in Hinny's hoose. Just two rooms, you know. But it was areet really. Room for me and Tilly, just. At night, they pushed two beds together for all us bairns. Head to toe, head to toe, head to toe. Matty, Bobby, Kenny, Willy, Eddy, Molly, Ruby, Lily, Milly, Sally, Tilly and – Barbara.'

'All in two beds?'

'Are you listening, or what? Barbara was the oldest. Nearest thing I've ever had to a sister. She told me all about how Old Jinny had tried to find out who'd lost Sally Salmon. I stayed with Hinny Carstairs till me teeth started falling out. That happens to all bairns. Orphans as well as proper ones. I would have been happy to stay longer, mind,' said Sally. 'But the wagman took us.'

'Wagman?'

'Howay, Tommy man, divvent say you've never heard of the wagman. It's the wagman's job to sniff oot bairns.'

'Is he a bad man?'

'Put it this way, if Stinkcross lived by that coaly river, he'd be a wagman. The wagman spends all day, every day, searching for bairns. Bairns that divvent gan to school. Bairns that divvent have nee proper homes. Bairns what neebody else wants. Bairns that live by playing the wag. Bairns like Sally Cats. The wagman snatched us on the coal staiths.'

'Coal staiths?'

'Divvent you know anything, Tom? The staiths is where the boats come for the coal. Made oot of wood, aren't they?

They stand in the river on massive stilts. Higher than the church where our Alleyman gadgie's plane crashed. Well, the wagman saw me hanging aboot Arnold's chippy one day. Arnold used to give me free chips and scraps. That's why I named the horse after him. Anyway, the wagman shouted: "Catch that runaway." So I ran away. Hid right at the top of the staiths. But he followed. Took the wagman and three bobbies to catch us. I would have jumped into the Tyne, but . . .'

'You can't swim.'

'They shoved me in a home. Words can be lies. It was aboot as much like a home as Miss Gently is gentle. A big, cold, draughty place on top of a hill. A home for them with nee home of their own.'

'An orphanage?' I asked. The word felt heavy as a stone.

Sally nodded. 'An orphanage asylum, they called it. Full of bairns neebody wanted. All of us slept in the same big dark room. But it wasn't nice like at Hinny Carstairs'. All of us had our meals in another big dark room. And all of us had lessons in *another* big dark room. If you could call them lessons. It was like being thrown doon a dark well — and just left there.'

At that moment we heard the faint *baa*ing of sheep — Scarcross was bringing his flock down from the fells.

8

'Scarcross is coming,' I said.

But Sally just sat there, eyes burning, as though she were back on those coal staiths — with the wagman and three bobbies coming for her.

'At the home,' she carried on, 'the authorities called us Sally Staiths. Luckily, I kept Tilly hidden — you weren't allowed to have anything of your own. You weren't allowed to do anything, or gan anywhere.'

'Weren't you ever allowed outside?'

'There was a yard. We were let out there sometimes. Then, every Sunday, people who wanted to adopt a bairn came to choose one; and the authorities would wash us, give us some clean clothes, comb our hair, and let us sit in a nice room — with a fire. Look nice and smile, the authorities told us, and mebbees you'll get a new mam and dad. A new mam and dad? It was what we all wanted. But I didn't get the chance. Thing is, Tommy man, the authorities didn't give me nee proper clothes, they didn't comb my hair, they didn't let me gan into the nice room to meet any new mams or dads.'

'Why not?'

Sally shrugged. 'They said neeone would want to adopt someone as wild as me. So when everyone else was meeting the new mams and dads, they just locked me in the darkest room of all — the coal cellar.'

The *baa*ing of sheep was growing louder. Scarcross was coming closer. Sally didn't seem to hear.

'But who's Ethel Kirkup?' I demanded. 'Who does the evacuee label belong to?'

Suddenly, Connie began to bark. The bleating of sheep filled the air. There was a thump. And another. The sheep were knocking against the side of the byre. Sally turned off her torch, plunging the hayloft into darkness. Scarcross was here. We heard him shouting and whistling as he moved the sheep into the drystone wall pen.

'Tune into your wirelesses tomorrow for episode two of the adventures of Sally Smith,' Sally whispered, imitating the voice of one of the radio announcers. 'And now, here's today's instalment of *Mr Stinkcross of Stinkcross Farm*, the amazing snake man.'

Connie was still barking when the door was kicked open and Scarcross strode into the byre below. 'I've a bone to pick with you, Geordie whelp,' he called up. 'First you took my cart; then you stole my whisky. And I told you not to let that horse out again, to eat its head off in me hayfield. Come down here, Missy Weasel, before I have to climb up there and get you.'

'Missy Weasel's not here,' Sally called back. 'Gan and look for her somewhere else.'

'You think it's a joke?' he snarled.

'Aye,' she grinned. 'I'm proper laughing me heed off.'

'Well let's see if you laugh at this.'

An object flew through the darkness and struck the edge of the hayloft door. Sally pulled me out of the way just in time. It was a hammer.

'Just wait until I get hold of you,' Scarcross threatened.

He began climbing the ladder. To my amazement, I heard Sally giggle. When Scarcross's head appeared in the opening, Sally's giggle became a burst of laughter.

'By God, I'm going to bring you into line, you pilfering little Tyneside rat,' Scarcross growled.

But before he could climb in, Scarcross found himself confronted by a blade.

'Climb back doon,' said Sally quietly, holding a large knife. 'Or get poked doon. It's up to you.'

Scarcross stared at the blade. In the poor light, he couldn't see what I could see — the eagle and swastika. It was the German airman's dagger.

Quick as the wing of a swallow, the dagger cut the air just inches from Scarcross's nose. Swearing loudly, he retreated and lumbered back outside.

'Told you I could handle Scaredycross,' Sally cried in triumph.

But the victory was short-lived. A few moments later,

Scarcross came back with his shotgun. He was shoving Silent Simon in front of him. Terrified, Silent Simon was trembling and wagging his finger, as though warning us not to come down.

'Right, Miss Wildcat,' shouted Scarcross. 'Drop that knife or this dunderhead is going for a swim.'

Cowering like a whipped dog, Silent Simon was dragged back outside. From the yard came the sound of a splash. Sally gasped. 'He's dunking Silent Simon. Like he did with the kittens.'

She shot down the ladder and darted through the byre door. I followed as quickly as I could. By the time I got onto the farmyard, Scarcross was holding Silent Simon's head down in the water butt. Silent Simon's boots kicked the air helplessly; his hands desperately clutching the rim of the barrel. Connie was barking. I had never heard her bark like this before — a snarling, blood curdling, matter-of-life-and-death kind of barking. Grabbing hold of Scarcross's trouser leg, Connie tried to drag him away.

'Get off, you mangy hound!' Scarcross yelled as his hobnailed boot kicked out and thudded into Connie's side.

Winded, Connie lay on the ground panting.

'Connie!' I cried, running over to her.

'You here an' all, young Thomas?' Scarcross growled.

In the confusion, Silent Simon had managed to break free. Scarcross picked up his gun and started after him. Sally ran over and stepped between the two of them.

'Leave him alone,' she ordered.

Scarcross's laughter lifted like a murder of crows.

'Thought that would flush you out, you Geordie sewer rat. Now it's your turn. I warned you when you interfered last time. Told you, it would be you in the water butt next.'

Breaking free from my hold, Connie hurled herself back at Scarcross. Scarcross swung his gun like a cricket bat, and hit her in the ribs.

Still growling, Connie slowly circled Scarcross. Scarcross's shotgun followed her. 'Connie,' I called again. 'Come here, girl.'

'Control that dog, or I'll fast shoot it,' he hissed.

'Here, girl,' I begged.

Limping over to me, Connie leaned heavily against my legs.

'Dangerous dogs have to be put down,' Scarcross said. 'I'm within my rights to destroy it.'

'You're the dangerous one,' Sally said. 'You should be destroyed.'

'For tuppence ha'penny, I'd shoot you as well,' Scarcross said, turning to point his shotgun at Sally.

'You wouldn't dare,' she challenged him.

Scarcross's face darkened. 'It's time for me to teach you a lesson you'll never forget.'

'You're just a bully,' said Sally.

'And you're just a townie toe-rag!' he shouted. 'If I did shoot you, no one would care.'

'Gan on then. Shoot me.' Sally was speaking quietly, but there was something in her tone that made Scarcross step back.

'Don't push me, lass,' he returned, his voice tight as a snare. 'You're just a wild animal yourself. Nowt more than vermin.'

'You can't kill me,' Sally said. 'Neebody can. I'm going to live to be a hundred!'

It all happened in an instant. Connie suddenly left my side and leapt at Scarcross. There was a deafening bang and a shower of falling sparks. The shotgun had been fired. When the smoke cleared, Sally was lying on the ground. Connie started howling.

'You've shot her,' I said, the smoke stinging my eyes. 'You've shot Sally.'

9

Sally lay on the ground. 'You shot her,' I repeated.

Rooted to the spot, I couldn't move. I couldn't think. All I could do was stare as the deafening gunshot kept echoing in my head. Scarcross couldn't move either. He was staring down at Sally too. Terrified, the sheep bleated wildly. Still howling, Connie nudged and pawed at me.

I don't know how long I stood like that for — it felt as though the whole world had stopped turning.

Then, someone was shouting. Faint at first, the voice got louder, until I could distinctly hear it over Connie and the sheep. 'Help! Help! Help!' It was coming from the direction of our house. Someone was running towards us round the tarn. It was Auntie Annie with Silent Simon. He was the one shouting: 'Help! Help! Help!'

Still bewildered, Scarcross hadn't moved.

'I didn't mean to,' he stammered. 'It was the dog's fault. It jumped at me. It was an accident.'

Scarcross bent down over Sally. When he was only inches

from her face, she sprang up like a Jack-in-the-box. Screaming, Scarcross stumbled backwards.

'What's going on?' Auntie Annie cried, suddenly running onto the farmyard. 'I heard a shotgun. What's happened?'

'It was him,' I gasped, pointing at Scarcross. 'He fired it.'

'Help! Help! Help!' Silent Simon cried over and over again, as though now that he'd found his voice, he couldn't keep quiet.

Auntie Annie ripped the shotgun from Scarcross's grip, and spinning round, hurled it away as far as she could.

'Mr Scarcross,' she demanded. 'What on earth is going on?'

'He tried to shoot Sally,' I stammered.

'Shoot Sally?' Auntie Annie repeated as though it was too much to understand. 'What do you mean, he tried to shoot Sally?'

'He fired at her,' I replied. 'Didn't he, Sally? He nearly killed you.'

Sally nodded. 'He only just missed.'

But Scarcross was quickly recovering. 'Thank the Lord you're here, Miss Grisedale,' he said. 'I'm afraid the children have got themselves over excited. You'll have heard my firearm being discharged. Well, we've had a bit of a to-do with yon dog.' He pointed at Connie. 'Came at me. Took a chunk out of me leg.'

'No, she didn't!' I protested.

'What's this then — Scotch mist?' Scarcross said, lifting a leg to show where Connie had torn his trousers. 'I had no choice but to shoot. Course, I aimed over the animal's head. Just wanted to frighten it off.'

'He's lying,' Sally said. 'Connie was just trying to protect me. She jumped at him to stop him from—'

'Shut your face!' Scarcross yelled. He turned back to Auntie Annie. 'That dog will have to be destroyed. You know as well as I do, Miss Grisedale, that if an animal's a wrong 'un, it has to be put down.'

'You're the wrong 'un,' Sally cried.

'That's enough, you Geordie scum,' Scarcross bellowed at Sally.

'Mr Scarcross,' Auntie Annie said. 'There's no need to talk to her like that.'

'She's my evacuee, I'll talk to her how I see fit,' Scarcross returned. 'You see, Miss Grisedale, an evacuee can't understand country ways, but we Woundale folk know that this dog's going to have to be put down. That's why I sent the lad to fetch you. With the hound belonging to your Thomas, I thought it a courtesy to let you destroy it.' Scarcross turned to Silent Simon. 'I told you to fetch Miss Grisedale, didn't I, lad?'

Silent Simon shook his head. 'Help! Help! Help!' he shouted, then ran off towards the sheep pens.

'Oh, take no notice of him,' Scarcross said. 'He's nowt but a halfwit.'

Auntie Annie went over to Sally and put a hand on her shoulder. 'You all right, pet?'

'He's the worst, nastiest, cruellest gadgie I've ever known,'

Sally said, staring at Scarcross. 'And I've met some proper monsters.'

Auntie Annie looked at Sally then at Scarcross. I could tell that something very rare was happening — she didn't know what to do.

'Cheeking your elders and betters again, are you?' Scarcross said. 'I'm afraid she gets like this a lot, Miss Grisedale. Doesn't know how to behave properly. I do my best with her. Try to stop her thieving little ways. Teach her right from wrong, but as you can see, it's a wasted job. And to think I fought the last war for the likes of her. Four years in a trench just to be cheeked by this. She's just flashed a knife at me, if you please. Where did she get that from, eh? A proper nasty weapon it was. Sharper than a bayonet. It's not one of mine. I'd check your tools if I were you. Well, this time I'm going to settle her. I tell you what, Miss Grisedale. You and young Thomas take yourselves home, and I'll deal with Missy Spitfire. And your dog too, if you want.'

'We'll look after our own dog, thank you very much, Mr Scarcross,' Aunt Annie replied coldly.

'As you like, Miss Grisedale. I just wanted to save you the upset.'

'And if you don't mind, Mr Scarcross,' Auntie Annie continued, 'I'll thank you to let us take young Sally as well.'

'Eh?' Scarcross demanded.

Auntie Annie had made up her mind: now she knew what to do. 'I'm taking Sally home with us.'

Scarcross pointed at his house. 'That's her home.'

'He makes her live in the byre,' I blurted.

'The byre?' Auntie Annie repeated.

I nodded vigorously. 'All winter in the byre, and he keeps her hungry.'

Auntie Annie crossed her arms. 'Come on, pet,' she said to Sally.

'She's not going anywhere,' Scarcross replied. 'She's my evacuee, Miss Grisedale. The law's on my side.'

'The thing is, Mr Scarcross,' Auntie Annie said, thinking quickly, 'we've a heap of sewing needs doing. And she's a whizz with the needle. So if you don't mind, we'll borrow her.'

'Well—' Scarcross said.

But Auntie Annie interrupted him. 'That's settled then. Have you got Connie, Tommy? Is she all right?'

I nodded. 'Seems to be.'

And before Scarcross could say anything else, Auntie Annie was hurrying us away, only stopping when we'd reached our own yard. 'I've never heard of anything like this before,' she said. 'Did he hurt you, Sally?'

Sally shrugged. 'Takes more than him to hurt me.'

'He tried to shoot her!' I cried. 'If Connie hadn't jumped on him, he might have killed her.'

'That's a very serious allegation, Tommy,' said Auntie Annie.

'But you heard him fire his shotgun,' I said.

'He said he fired it over Connie's head,' Auntie Annie said.

'And he whacked Connie,' I cried. 'Connie didn't bite him. Sally's right. He's the cruellest, nastiest, horriblest—'

'That's enough for now,' Auntie Annie said sharply. 'We'll sort it all out in the morning.'

'You're not going to do it, are you?' I asked, my voice feeling tight.

'Do what?' Auntie Annie asked.

'Destroy Connie?' I said.

'If she's bitten Mr Scarcross then I'll have to, Tom. No matter what. You know that as well as I do.'

I felt myself choking. 'She was only trying to stop him from—'

Before I could explain, my other aunties appeared at the back door. 'What's happening?' Auntie Dolly asked.

'What's the to do?' Auntie Gladys pressed.

'Is it the German airman?' Auntie Gladys and Auntie Dolly asked at the same time.

'Oh, for goodness' sake, if I hear anything more about a German airman,' Auntie Annie snapped. 'Sally's come to stay. She can sleep with Vi and Gladys tonight. I'll sort everything else in the morning. Now stop blethering, everyone.'

There was something in the tone of Auntie Annie's voice that made my other aunties fall silent.

'Upstairs, love,' Auntie Annie told Sally gently.

'What about the sewing?' Sally asked.

'There isn't any.'

'I can work,' said Sally. And all at once she began to beg: 'If you let me stay here, I'll work every hour God sends. I'll do all your sewing and the milking and the hens and . . .'

'I just want you to have a good night's sleep,' said Auntie Annie. 'And nothing else.'

I stayed in the kitchen as Auntie Annie led Sally upstairs.

Sally's tread on the worn stairs sounded strange. When you know a house well, you get to recognise all the creaks and groans, and who or what makes them. And nowhere is this truer than on stairs. Everyone makes their own unique sound going up and then coming down. It's like a signature, or fingerprint. Maybe you don't really know someone until you can recognise their tread on the stairs.

I could tell that both of my aunts were desperate to question me about what had happened. But they also both knew that Auntie Annie didn't want them to. I rolled up my shirt sleeves and went to put my boots back on.

'Where do you think you're going, Thomas Grisedale?' Auntie Annie demanded, as she came back downstairs.

'I've the nettles to scythe,' I said.

'Don't worry about that tonight.'

'Auntie Annie?' I blurted.

'What is it, Tom?'

'Don't believe a word Scarcross says, he—'

'That's *Mr* Scarcross to you, young man. You and Sally are just children; I think you'd do well to remember that. Now get some sleep, lad. I'll sort it all out in the morning.'

10

Sort it all out in the morning. But could Auntie Annie really sort out everything that needed sorting out?

Sitting on my windowsill, I stared through the window at Woundale. We weren't far from Midsummer's Eve, and the light seemed to take forever to fade.

I could hear the sound of penned sheep — someone had brought another flock down. Closer at hand came the rhythmic swish of the scythe as Auntie Annie cut the nettles. I could hear my other aunties in the kitchen.

'What do you think happened?' Auntie Dolly was saying.

'It must have been bad,' Auntie Gladys replied. 'I've never seen Simon so worked up.'

'And him talking again after all these years,' said Auntie Dolly.

'Did you see how upset our Tom was? He's not one to cry wolf.'

'Sally too. Poor mite, she put a brave face on it, but I could see she was shaking. I know you think she's wild, Glad, but she's just a bairn. A bairn with no one to look out for her.'

Auntie Gladys sighed, 'I know, Doll. And you know what else? Even our Annie doesn't quite know what to do.'

'Well, whatever's happened, we'll find out soon enough.'

'Aye, it'll all come out in the wash tomorrow morning.'

What would happen tomorrow? Sitting on the windowsill, I wondered whether we'd be going to school, or helping with the shearing? The Woundale annual clipping was a tradition. I'd never missed it before. And what about Connie? At least she wasn't badly hurt. If Auntie Annie knew the truth, she'd never let Connie be destroyed. But would she believe us? Grown-ups usually just believe other grown-ups.

My aunties continued talking, but I was no longer listening. Sometime later, I heard the front door open as Auntie Annie came back in. She mounted the stairs. A creak on a floorboard told me that she had gone to Vi and Sally's room. There was a moment's pause. Then she was passing back down the stairs.

'How's Sally?' I heard Auntie Gladys ask.

'Fast asleep,' replied Auntie Annie.

'Poor little bairn,' said Auntie Dolly.

'One thing I have found out,' Auntie Annie told them. 'She's been sleeping in Mr Scarcross's filthy byre since she came here.'

'What?' Auntie Gladys gasped.

'So tonight's her first time in a proper bed since she got to Woundale?' Auntie Dolly asked.

'For all we know she might never have been in a proper bed,' added Auntie Gladys.

'She's more a slave than an evacuee,' put in Auntie Dolly.

'I've been remiss,' Auntie Annie decided. 'I ought to have stood up to Mr Scarcross. I shouldn't have taken no for an answer. I should have forced him to let her live here with us.'

'But how could you do that?' asked Auntie Gladys. 'She's his evacuee.'

'Oh, that Scarcross is a bad lot all together,' said Auntie Dolly.

'No, Dolly,' said Auntie Annie more gently. 'Not all together bad. It was the last war that turned him that way. Before that he wasn't so different from anyone else. Happen he lost more than his eye in the trenches. He left his better part behind on that Somme battlefield. Came back all angry. Bitter. Twisted. And he's been that shape ever since. I've always felt a bit sorry for him. My young man was friends with him when they all joined up. He'd been all right then.'

There was a silence — I'd never heard Auntie Annie mention her young man before.

'And what about our Arthur?' wondered Auntie Dolly at last. 'Will he be all bitter and twisted if he comes back?'

'There's some folks that have it in them to get back into their proper shape,' returned Auntie Annie. 'No matter what happens. And I fancy our Arthur is one of them.'

'Well, I hope he does come back,' said Auntie Gladys. 'Our Tommy is missing him something awful. He hasn't been himself these past few days.'

'Aye well,' yawned Auntie Annie. 'We'll have to be getting to bed now ourselves. Sheep clipping tomorrow.'

At that moment Connie began to bark. A volley of knocking rapped against the door.

'Who is it?' I heard Auntie Annie call.

'It's me, Miss Grisedale,' a familiar voice returned.

'We're about to go to bed, Mr Scarcross,' Auntie Annie answered.

'I know it's late, ladies,' Scarcross said. 'But I think there's something you'll want to know about yon lass you're harbouring.'

Hearing Auntie Annie open the door, I waited for Scarcross's footsteps in the hall, but Auntie Annie hadn't invited him in. I could hear what they were saying through my open window.

'I feel it only right and proper to warn you, Miss Grisedale,' Scarcross said. 'You're mollycoddling an adder with that lying evacuee.'

'What can you mean, Mr Scarcross?' came Auntie Annie's cold reply.

'Well, as I've told you, this evening she lunged at me with a knife. And I've just found out that she attacked a boy at school today. Came within a ha'penny of killing him.'

'What kind of cock-and-bull story is that?' Auntie Annie demanded impatiently.

'It's the truth,' he growled. 'She wrestled the butcher's lad to the ground and bit his ear off.'

'Quite frankly,' said Auntie Annie, 'I'm surprised at you, making up stories like that.'

'You don't need to take my word for it,' said Scarcross. 'It's all round town. I've been talking to Rebanks and some of the other shepherds. They told me Sally brayed the butcher's lad at school today. And right in the schoolyard, thank you very much.'

'Are you finished, Mr Scarcross?' Auntie Annie said, in the crossest voice I'd ever heard her use to another grown-up.

'No, I'm not. Apparently after biting the butcher's lad's ear off, she decked Miss Gently — knocked her clean to the ground. And then there was a break in. In the staffroom. Townsfolk are saying it was the Alleyman airman, but if you ask me, it was that evacuee. She's as crooked as a dog's hind leg. Oh, you'll find out for yourself soon enough, Miss Grisedale. Miss Gently has already gone to the police. Sergeant Collinson will likely be calling on you. I'll be sure to let him know about her thieving ways here in Woundale. And there's one last thing just to cap it all off.'

'Really?'

'I have reason to know that she's a runaway.'

'A runaway?'

'Turns out they think she absconded from the orphan asylum. The authorities have been looking for her. Only just tracked her down. I hear they want all the absconders taken to a special institution. Sergeant Collinson will want to make inquiries as to that as well. No doubt, he'll be coming to

Woundale to take her away. So if you don't mind, I'll take her into secure custody now. Before she can run away again.'

'Well, I do mind,' cried Auntie Annie.

'Eh?'

'The way you've treated that little lass is nothing short of disgraceful. In fact, I've decided that she's not staying another minute with you. You're not fit to have an evacuee. She lives here now. I'm taking responsibility for her.'

'You can't do that.'

'That's exactly what I am doing, Mr Scarcross. And if you don't like it, you can lump it.'

'Well, we'll see what the law says, shall we? When Collinson arrests her as a runaway and a juvenile delinquent.'

After Scarcross had stumped away, swearing to himself, I waited for my aunts to start talking again. But matters were too serious for chatter. Slowly, Connie's barking quietened. In the silence, I heard my aunties climb the stairs to bed. Then, there was only me awake and the tawny owls calling to each other in the woods. I put the blackout curtains up and got into bed.

11

I hadn't been lying in bed for long when my door opened.

'Get up, Tommy,' I heard Sally whisper.

'Why?'

'Got to finish what we started, haven't we?'

And before I could ask her what she meant, or tell her what I had heard about Sergeant Collinson, Sally was disappearing me down the stairs and slipping out into the night.

Sally led us round the tarn. 'Where are we going?' I asked.

'To Snakecross's.'

'We aren't.'

'We are.'

'We can't.'

'We have to.'

'Why?' My question was so loud that a heron, hunting in the night-time tarn, gave a loud *crark!* and lumbered away on its wings.

'Got to get something from the byre.'

'Are you joking?'

'I've never joked less in me life.'

'And what if Scarcross catches us?'

'He never gans in the byre, unless he's coming after me, and he knows I'm at yours.'

'If it's Tilly you're going for,' I replied, 'we'll tell Auntie Annie and she'll come and get it tomorrow.'

'This is even more important than Tilly. And if I lose it, I've lost everything. Howay, we can be in and out in a jiffy.'

'What is it you'll lose?'

'The most important thing in the universe, and I have to get it now cos Scarecross will chuck all me stuff out in the morning. Come on, Tommy, they only leave the food cupboard unlocked for a moment. If you don't take your chance, you starve.'

'Food cupboard? What are you on about?' I demanded.

'It's now or never.'

Sally continued alone.

'Don't go, Sally.'

'I have to, I have to rescue her.'

'Rescue who?'

'Sally Smith, that's who! Come with and you'll understand. Howay, we'll be in and out as quick as a pair of weasels.'

We ran across the Scarcross farmyard, and darted into the byre. Arnold welcomed her with a snort.

'Whisht, Arnold,' Sally said and she shot up the hayloft ladder.

Standing at the foot of the ladder, I could hear the mice

scurrying in the hay above. Then I climbed up after her. She was sitting in the hay, with her torch switched on, staring at a big brown envelope.

'These are me records,' she whispered. 'From the orphanage. Just before I ran away, I broke into the office and swiped them.'

'Ran away?'

'Why aye, ran away, Tommy man. Do you think I'd stay in that prison a moment longer than I had to?' She opened the envelope and unfolded a sheet of paper. 'This is what I had to come back for. You see, the authorities lied. They told me neebody would ever want us, but it says here that somebody did. They even came to the orphanage looking for us. Somebody wanted me, but they were sent packing.'

'Who came for you?' I asked.

'That's where I need your help, bonny lad.' Sally handed me the paper. 'Since Auntie Annie's been helping me to read, I've been able to understand some of it. But there's a bit I still cannet work oot. The important bit.'

I went and sat beside her. Sally shone the torch on the sheet of paper. The handwriting was difficult to read. Most of it seemed to be a record of her punishments, and a list of the times she'd run away. Sometimes she'd been gone for nights on end. I read out loud the bit that had been underlined: 'Sally Staiths is a feral child and not fit for adoption.'

'I know what feral means,' Sally grinned. 'It means they

couldn't tame us. But I divvent care about any of that. It's this bit I cannet make oot.'

She turned the page over and brought the torch nearer. The bright beam found a scrawl of smudged, spidery handwriting.

Slowly, I deciphered the scribbled note: '10th July 1936,' I read. 'A disreputable character came to the orphanage door, inquiring about the troublemaker Sally Staiths.'

'Disreputable character,' she asked. 'Does that mean a bad gadgie?'

'I'm not sure, I think so.'

'Probably means they're a good egg then. The authorities always twist everything round from the proper way. Howay, get on with it.'

I continued to read: 'An Alleyman mariner by the sound of him.'

'I found out what Alleyman is for myself,' Sally whispered.

'A German,' I breathed. 'And a mariner is a sailor.'

'I guessed that from the next bit. Carry on, Tom.'

'We sent him packing back to his ship,' I read on. 'He was claiming p—' I broke off.

'Claiming?' Sally asked breathlessly. 'What was the Alleyman sailor claiming?'

'I don't know. Pat something.'

'Pat Something, who's he?'

'I don't think it's a name.'

'What is it then?'

'I can't read it. The handwriting is shocking.'

'Try spelling it oot.'

I cleared my throat. 'He was claiming pat . . . ern . . . ity.'

'What does pat . . . ern . . . ity mean?'

'I don't know,' I replied. 'I've never heard that word before.'

There was another long silence. Sally put her records carefully back into their envelope. 'There's only one thing for it,' she said and, slipping the envelope into one of her big pockets, shot back down the ladder.

But when I followed her onto the farmyard, I couldn't see her. The water barrel stood menacingly in the moonlight. Then I saw a stab of torchlight flashing against the grey farmhouse.

'Psst,' Sally called over from Scarcross's house door.

I hurried over.

'We're not going in?' I breathed in horror.

'There's something in there that I need. Just one last thing.'

'But he's just tried to shoot you.'

'I keep on telling you not to worry aboot Skunkcross,' she replied. 'Listen.'

She turned her torch off and we stood there in the moonlight.

'Can't you hear?' she whispered.

The sound of Scarcross's snoring came from his open bedroom window.

'Oot for the count,' said Sally. 'I'm always letting myself

in when I hear him snoring. Once Snoutcross has gone to the land of nod you couldn't even wake him up if you wrung a wet dish clout over his face.'

She reached out and tried the door. It was locked.

'That's it,' I said. 'Let's leg it.'

'You still divvent understand, do you?'

'No, I don't.'

'Then listen to us, Tommy man. I've spent me life being banged up and put away. So, when I find a locked door, sometimes I just cannet help meself — I have to unlock it. If they want to keep me oot, I have to gan in. If they want to keep us in a cage; I have to fly oot through the bars. And if Scarcross won't let us in the hoose, then into the hoose I'll gan. You'd feel the same way if you were me. Besides, I really need what he's got. He locks the door to keep me oot, but I know where he hides the spare.' She plucked up a stick and swiped it across the lintel above the door. A key fell to the ground. Sally snatched it up. 'So, are you coming in with us or not?'

All at once I thought of Sally being shut in the orphanage coal cellar when all the would-be mams and dads came looking for someone to adopt.

'Are you sure he won't wake up, Sal?'

'You could fry chips in his greasy hair and he wouldn't budge.'

Auntie Annie's words came into my mind — all alonc in the world.

'I'm coming in with you,' I decided.

'Champion,' she beamed. 'You're the best friend I've ever had.'

Sally turned the key in the lock. It clicked. She switched on her torch. The door creaked open. We tiptoed in.

The house was silent except for the loud rumbling from Scarcross's bedroom.

'Snorecross,' Sally whispered, then scrunched her face up and grunted like Mavis.

The Eveready torch guided us down a musty hallway.

'It's in here,' Sally urged, carefully opening another door.

She led me into Scarcross's back parlour. The torch beam found a huge table right in the middle of the room. It only had one chair. A single cup was placed in front of the chair. Sally went straight over. One of the table legs was wonky. A book had been wedged underneath to keep it steady.

'Howay,' urged Sally. 'Lift it up for us.'

The table was heavy but I just managed to lift it enough for Sally to reach down and yank the book free. As I lowered the table, I could do nothing to stop the cup rolling off and smashing onto the stone flagged floor.

The sound felt loud as a shout.

'Why divvent you just gan upstairs and hammer on his door?' Sally murmured.

I waited for Scarcross to wake, but Sally was already flipping through the book. 'It's a dictionary,' she explained. 'P for pat ... ern ... ity,' she mumbled. 'P for pat ... ern ... ity.'

To my great relief, the snoring continued to boom out from above.

It was a very old dictionary. No one had opened it for years, and as Sally turned the thin pages, motes of dust rose and swirled in her torch beam.

'J, K, L, M,' she whispered. 'N, O, Q.'

'You've missed P,' I pointed out.

Sally thrust the dictionary at me. 'Here, Mr Know-it-all, you find it then.'

Licking my finger to separate the thin pages, I turned back to P. Carefully, I scanned down the long list of words until: 'Pat-ern-ity,' I announced.

'What does it mean?' Sally gasped.

'Hold the torch steady and bring it closer,' I ordered. 'It means,' I said, putting my finger under the definition and slowly reading the small print. 'The state of being . . .'

'Get a move on,' Sally begged, 'the state of being what?'

'The state of being . . .' I continued, 'someone's father.'

'What?'

'It means the Alleyman said he was your dad.'

For a moment Sally showed no reaction. Then her face lit up even more brightly than the torch beam. I had never seen her look so happy. 'I always knew it,' she whispered, 'deep doon, I always knew I wasn't nee orphan. Always knew someone wanted us. That Alleyman sailor was my dad.'

'Well, he said he was.'

Sally began to dance. She danced round and round the

room, waving the torch, flinging her arms up joyfully and kicking her legs higher and higher. Suddenly there was a deafening crash. She'd kicked the broken cup so hard that it had smashed against the skirting board. In the terrible silence that followed, I realised that the snoring had stopped. Then we heard a heavy tread on the floorboards above us. 'Who's down there?' Scarcross shouted.

We darted out of the parlour and back down the hall. In no time at all we were sprinting over the yard and round the tarn. By the time Scarcross saw the table, the dictionary and the smashed cup, we would be long gone. With any luck, he'd think the table had fallen. But for now, neither of us cared about Scarcross. We were just so happy for Sally. She wasn't an orphan!

Sally and I parted on the stairs. 'The rainbow was right,' she smiled. 'Everything is going to be all right. I'm like you now, Tom. I've got a dad. I've got someone who wants me after all.'

'You know what, Sal?' I said. 'Auntie Annie's got a dictionary.'

Stifling our laughter, we crept back to our bedrooms.

I lay awake in the dark. For a long time, I couldn't stop smiling about how happy Sally was. But one by one, all our problems seemed to gather around me in the darkness like ghosts. What if Connie got destroyed? What about Miss Gently and the first aid kit? What if the airman really was part of the invasion? And I still hadn't warned Sally about what I'd heard Scarcross say about Sergeant Collinson. They knew Sally was a runaway, they were looking for her. No doubt he'd come to take her away.

Half a dozen times I decided to go and wake Auntie Annie up now and tell her about the airman, and about everything else. Wasn't that the only way out of this whole mess? But I'd promised Sally that I'd keep the secret. A promise might only weigh a few words, but sometimes it can get too heavy to carry.

METHERA ...

1

I was woken next morning by Connie jumping on my bed and licking me.

'Connie!' I cried, burying my face into her lovely soft flank.

She was still alive! And she didn't seem to be too sore either. For a moment I was just happy to be with my dog. Then all the troubles of the night returned.

'Thomas,' Auntie Annie called up the stairs. 'Breakfast's ready.'

When I saw the grandfather clock, I could hardly believe my eyes. It was nearly eight o'clock. I couldn't remember the last time I'd slept in that late. No one else was around.

'I'm letting Sally sleep a bit longer too,' Auntie Annie said.

I took the bowl she was holding out. Through the open house door, we could hear the blare of sheep in the shearing pens.

'Special treat,' she said. 'Bread and bacon dripping. You'll need the energy. We've a hard day's work ahead of us. We've sorted the flocks. The Hawkriggs came at first light. Auntie Gladys and Auntie Dolly have already started clipping.'

Auntie Annie laid another plate on the breakfast table and,

going to the house door, called onto the yard: 'You can come in, love. Breakfast's ready.' Then she dropped her voice to me. 'Silent Simon slept in the woods last night. He's been helping us this morning.'

And in shambled Silent Simon.

'Don't worry, pet,' Auntie Annie told him. 'No one's going to hurt you here. We'll make you a shake-me-down for tonight. There's going to be some changes in Woundale. You just work with us today. You're one of us now.'

The breakfast was delicious, but as I ate it, I could feel Auntie Annie looking at me as though she couldn't wait to start asking me questions. When Silent Simon finished, he smiled and then hurried off to help Auntie Gladys and Auntie Dolly with the clipping.

I had to get away too, before Auntie Annie could start interrogating me. If only I could tell her everything, but I couldn't until Sally had agreed.

'Right,' said Auntie Annie sitting down at the kitchen table. 'I've made a pot of tea. I think the best way is if you tell me everything.'

'Everything?' I returned, barely able to get the word out.

Auntie Annie nodded. 'Everything.'

If only I could tell her everything.

'Now,' Auntie Annie began. 'Mr Scarcross came round last night. Made all sorts of allegations about Sally. I want the truth. So let's begin with what happened at school yesterday.'

I took a deep breath, and then told Auntie Annie about how Bertie Tupperman bullied the whole class, but seemed to hate Sally the most, making up songs about her and getting everyone to join in. I told her what happened when Sally was playing hopscotch.

'Bertie Tupperman spat at her?' Auntie Annie asked.

'Yes, a huge gobful.'

'So she bit him?' Auntie Annie continued.

'He deserved it,' I replied, 'everyone in the class said so. Everyone was glad she did it.'

'And did Sally knock Miss Gently down?'

'Miss Gently always picks on her,' I explained. 'Yesterday she nearly shook Sally's head off and—'

'What about the theft from the staffroom?' Auntie Annie interrupted.

I felt my stomach twist.

'Tommy, did Sally break into the staffroom?'

In order to avoid a direct lie, I quickly described Miss Gently searching the girls' bags and how she couldn't find any stolen goods. I didn't mention the first aid kit. I wasn't lying, I just wasn't telling the whole truth.

'Miss Jameson had to slap Miss Gently to make her stop shaking Sally,' I went on.

'And Sally had nothing to do with the theft?'

Auntie Annie looked me directly in the eye. I'd once heard my dad say that in war the first casualty is the truth, and now I think I knew what he meant.

'Thomas,' Auntie Annie pressed. 'I'm asking you. Is Sally a thief?'

I shook my head, trying to hide just how miserable it felt to be deceiving her.

Auntie Annie nodded. 'Thank you for telling me the truth. I believe you. I know what Miss Gently is like. I was at school with her myself.'

In the silence that followed, Auntie Annie poured us each a cup of milky tea. 'Now, tell me what happened with Mr Scarcross yesterday. What's all this about a knife?'

'He threw a hammer at us,' I said, trying to evade lying about the knife.

'A hammer?'

'It nearly hit us. And then he ducked Silent Simon in the water butt, pretending to drown him, like the kittens.'

'What kittens?'

'He hit Connie. Then he fired his gun.'

Auntie Annie sat up straight. 'Do you really think he meant to shoot her?'

'I thought so,' I returned. 'I don't know now. It all happened so quickly. Maybe he was trying to scare off Connie. But he's always doing nasty things and he will shoot someone someday. And Sally's got no one to look out for her.'

'You've got to tell me everything, you know, Tom. If I'm going to help Sally, you can't keep anything back. You see, I've been told she's a runaway — from an orphanage. Is that true?'

I took a gulp of tea, and then the words came tumbling out. I described how Sally was found in the River Tyne and stayed first with Old Auntie Jinny and after that, Hinny Carstairs. I told her how the wagman snatched her on the coal staiths. I explained that they put her in a coal cellar and never let her get picked by a new mam and dad. And before I could stop myself I was telling her how one day an Alleyman mariner came to the orphanage to claim her.

'A German sailor?' Auntie Annie was puzzled. 'Is that why she asked me what an Alleyman was?'

I nodded. 'Could her dad be a German sailor?'

'I suppose, it's possible, Tom. There was a lot of toing and froing between England and Germany after the last war. And right up till recently. Especially in ports like Tyneside.'

'So, maybe Sally's half-German,' I said.

'For goodness' sake don't let Mr Scarcross hear you say that, Thomas. So she is a runaway — and an orphan.' She tightened the knot on her headscarf. 'So how on earth did she get to Woundale?'

'I don't know. She brought her records with her. That's how she found out about the Alleyman.'

Then I heard myself describe Sally's life on the Scarcross farm. How she was not only locked in the byre in all weathers, but half-starved and made to do all the work. Suddenly, I realised that if I kept talking, any moment now I was going to tell Auntie Annie about the German airman.

I must have stopped myself just in time, because all at

once there was silence and only the clock ticking, and the sound of sheep bleating.

'All right, Tommy,' Auntie Annie said. 'You'd best get off to the clipping.'

'What about Connie?'

Auntie Annie's reply was to do something she rarely did. She threw her arms round me and gave me a hug as deep as the tarn. 'No one's going to lay a finger on our Connie, do you hear me? I know now that Connie was just trying to protect you. What would the Woundale Clipping be without that dog?'

'What about Sally?' I asked. 'What's going to happen to her?'

At that moment, we heard Sally's feet coming down the stairs.

2

If hugging me was a rarity, I'd never seen Auntie Annie so much as shake Sally's hand before. But the moment she came into the kitchen, Auntie Annie swept her into her arms.

I thought that it would make Sally uncomfortable, or that she might even struggle to get free. I was wrong. She folded into Auntie Annie as though she were Tilly, the rag doll.

I could see how happy Sally was, but when she caught my eye, she put her tongue out.

'Right, lass, eat up,' said Auntie Annie. 'We just use our fingers for today's breakfast. It's a special treat. You'll need it, we're sheep shearing.'

'No school?' Sally asked.

'No school,' said Auntie Annie. 'It's the Woundale Clipping. And you just leave Mr Scarcross to me.'

Sitting down at the kitchen table, Sally dipped her hunk of bread into the bowl of bacon dripping, and began scooping it out hungrily. When she'd finished the bread, she licked the bowl clean. 'Thanks, Auntie Annie,' she said. 'That was fit for the King.' She handed back the clean bowl. 'And look, I've already done the washing up.'

Our laughter rang out through the kitchen.

'Now,' said Auntie Annie. 'Time to clip them sheep.'

Linking arms, Auntie Annie marched us round the tarn to the field where our sheep were penned.

'Perfect weather for the Woundale Clipping,' she said, looking up at the deep blue sky over the dale.

Maybe she really would be able to sort things out.

Connie kept close to my ankles, ready to work. As we walked, Sally recited the poem about the cloud, trying to make her voice sound like she was Woundale born and bred. She'd learnt it off by heart. We laughed until our sides hurt.

'We don't talk like that, lass,' grinned Auntie Annie.

'Aye, happen you do, lass,' replied Sally.

We were still laughing when we arrived. I was glad because I realised this was Auntie Annie's way of showing Scarcross that she was on our side. But it meant I hadn't been able to warn Sally about Sergeant Collinson. And there wasn't time to talk now either.

The whole dale seemed filled with sheep, and they all needed clipping. Some of the sheep had a red S daubed on their side. This was their smit mark and meant that they belonged to Scarcross. Mr Rebanks's flocks were smit-marked with a black R on their shoulder. The sheep marked with a red H on their haunch were owned by the Hawkriggs. There were a good few other flocks too, from the nearby fell farms. Most of them were Herdwick sheep, bred to live in the fells. We called them the smiling sheep, because they always looked so happy. Our sheep were marked with a red G. I felt a burst of pride at seeing them all together — to me they looked like the best sheep from all the fells. When we got nearer, their bleating almost drowned out everything else, even the sound of the cuckoo calling from the woods. Auntie Gladys and Auntie Dolly had already started. So had the shepherds, including Mr Rebanks. Emily Rebanks had come with him. She often helped her dad at busy times. The other fell farmers were hard at work, including the Hawkriggs. Scarcross was shearing at a distance away from everyone else.

'You two come and work with Simon and Emily,' Auntie Annie called and took us over to the drystone pen where our sheep were gathered. Both of them had large crooks. Emily's crook was taller than she was; she waved it in greeting at Sally. Connie nudged me, waiting eagerly for the order to begin work.

Sally looked into the pen. 'That's a gimmer,' she said, pointing at a young female sheep.

'Aye it is,' said Emily.

'Gummer,' Sally added, indicating a very old yowe with no teeth. Then she pointed at a larger sheep with a set of curled horns. 'And there's Mr Tup,' she cried. 'Tups are boy sheep. And they'll knock you into next week if you're not careful.'

'Ee,' said Auntie Annie. 'We'll make a Woundale lass of you yet.'

'Tommy taught us all about sheep when we had to dig them out of the snow last winter,' said Sally. 'But why's that one asleep?' she asked, gesturing at the biggest, woolliest yowe that was lying on its back with its legs in the air.

'It's rigged,' I said.

'Riggweltered,' nodded Auntie Annie. 'The poor thing's upturned and it can't right itself because the fleece is too heavy.'

'Well, somebody needs to help it then,' said Sally. 'Come on, Emily.'

Sally and Emily vaulted the wall, and dropped into the pen. Wriggling through the press of sheep, they helped the riggweltered yowe to spring back onto its feet.

'By, but you're a natural,' said Auntie Annie. 'Now we'll have to teach her how to count, won't we, Emily?'

Emily grinned.

'Will you two tally the sheep and then collect the fleeces?' Auntie Annie went on.

Sally beamed. 'Leave it to us land girls.'

'And Tommy,' Auntie Annie continued. 'I think with help from Simon, you'll be able to do a bit of clipping this year.'

Last year, I'd helped my dad. But I was a year stronger.

'Sally, I've got to tell you something,' I whispered when Auntie Annie had gone to clip with my other aunties in one of the other pens.

'Not now,' she shot back.

'It's important.'

'Can't you see the land girls have got work to do. There's a war on, don't you know?'

I went with Simon to one of the temporary pens, a square made out of wooden wicker hurdles. It was in here that we'd be doing our clipping.

'When I say now,' I called to Emily and Sally. 'Let the first lot out.'

'Aye, aye, sir,' Sally saluted.

Emily grinned at Sally.

'Connie will drive them through to us,' I instructed.

Connie crouched low at my ankles, desperate for the command.

'Howay, man,' Sally returned. 'Get on with it.'

'Right, we'll start now,' I called, moving aside one of our hurdles so there was room for the sheep to enter our pen.

Sally and Emily lifted away the slate covering the hogg hole. The hogg hole was the gap in the drystone wall through which sheep could pass. A hogg being a sheep that hadn't been sheared yet.

Counting sheep isn't as easy as it sounds. You have to do it very carefully, or you soon lose the tally. Maybe this was why we always used special sheep numbers — somehow it was easier than the usual way of counting: 'Yan, tan, tethera,' Emily counted as she and Sally released the first three sheep.

'Walk up, Connie,' I whispered, giving her the command to approach the sheep calmly.

'Methera, pimp, sethera, lethera,' Emily continued — four, five, six, seven.

'Hovera, dovera, dick,' we both chorused — eight, nine, ten.

'Yan-a-dick, tan-a-dick, tethera-a-dick, methera-a-dick,' Emily counted — eleven, twelve, thirteen, fourteen. 'Bumfit.'

'Bumfit?' Sally burst out laughing.

'That's fifteen,' beamed Emily, then very quickly: 'Yan-a-bumfit, tan-a-bumfit, tethera-a-bumfit.' — sixteen, seventeen, eighteen.

'Methera-a-bumfit, giggot,' we finished together — nineteen, twenty.

Connie was already moving the sheep towards us.

I whistled sharply between my fingers, something all fell farmers know how to do, and Connie guided the sheep a little to the right so they wouldn't miss our opening. But she moved them too much, so I whistled again, this time giving two wavering notes. Then I shouted. 'Come by.'

And with that Connie righted the direction of the sheep so they passed into the pen. I quickly shut them in.

Sally was still laughing as she came over. 'Bumfit!' she giggled. 'And you lot say I talk funny. Bumfit!'

Selecting a quiet old gummer, Simon laid her down and held her legs. Then he handed me the clippers.

'Do you want me to start?' I asked.

'You start,' he nodded.

And we both smiled to hear him speak.

Everything my dad had taught me last year came back to me now. *Give her a little stroke on the face so she knows you're a friend.* Reaching out, I stroked the old gummer reassuringly. *Start with the neck and keep the skin tight, so as not to nick her.* I began to clip the gummer's neck.

'Good,' Simon encouraged.

Under Simon's guiding hand, I was clipping her back when the old yowe suddenly wriggled. *If she gets a bit het up, maybe tell her what you're doing,* my dad had said. 'I'm just taking your fleece off,' I whispered into the sheep's ear. 'So you can be nice and cool.' She quietened.

When it came to the belly wool, I let Simon take over and he showed me how to keep the fleece whole.

I quickly glanced down the dale. Thankfully, Scarcross was still keeping his distance. Through the corner of my eye, I could see that he was clipping alone, well away from everyone else. Then I looked up at the road coming down into the dale. No sign of Sergeant Collinson. Maybe he wouldn't come today. He'd know the Woundale Clipping had started.

'You can finish her,' said Simon, not silent now.

I'd just started clipping the gummer again, when I heard a burst of giggling. Looking up, I saw Sally and Emily watching me.

'You missed a bit,' Sally said. 'Howay, Tommy Tortoise. Want me to show you how to dee it quicker?'

Clipping always takes longer when someone's watching. But at last, I finished. Released from Simon's grip, our first sheared sheep of the year bounded away. Without her fleece, she looked half the size she'd been before.

Sally roared with laughter. 'Look at her, she's been shrunk in the laundry!' Then vaulting a hurdle, Sally dropped down into the pen. Emily followed. They began 'skirting' the fleece, taking off the bits of whin, burrs and dung entangled in the wool. I was desperate to talk to Sally, but they'd soon rolled up the fleece and were already taking it to the cart. Simon had chosen another gummer for us.

3

Simon and I worked well together. But my arms and back soon ached. With every passing minute it got hotter. Blinded by sweat, it wasn't long before I'd forgotten what Scarcross might say or do. Forgotten about Sally being a runaway. Forgotten even to scan the road into Woundale for Sergeant Collinson's bicycle. All I wanted to do was to stop clipping and jump into the tarn to cool off. To give me a break, Simon did a few of the livelier gimmers and hoggs on his own.

'I wish I was that quick,' I said.

'One day,' Simon nodded.

'Another lot of yan, tan, tethera?' Sally shouted.

And Connie was soon driving more sheep our way.

Just when I thought I couldn't work one more minute, I heard Auntie Annie calling: 'Bait-time!'

She brought over a basket full of buttered bread, hardboiled eggs, some tomatoes and billycans of refreshing cold tea. We took it to a birch tree and sat down. We were so hungry we didn't even mind that our hands were all greasy from handling the wool, and we stuffed our faces and guzzled the tea until it ran down our chins. The grown-ups ate their bait under a large rowan tree.

The dogs had waded into the tarn and were drinking deeply. Then, tongue lolling, and sides heaving, Connie came over to join us. It was lovely and cool in the dappled shade. The sheep had quietened and now we could hear the cuckoo calling from the woods.

I really had to talk to Sally now. Warn her. Even if Emily heard me. What if Sergeant Collinson did come today? Maybe he was already on his way.

'Listen, Sally,' I began. 'I've got something serious to tell you—'

'I know,' Sally interrupted. 'Emily's already told me. Haven't you, Emily?'

'Yes,' said Emily.

'Told you what?' I shot back.

'That the bobbies are after us. She heard Miss Gently talking to Bertie Rubberman's dad, didn't you, Emily?'

'Yes,' Emily repeated.

Sally shrugged. 'Bobbies divvent worry me. I can handle any copper, me.'

'Miss Gently said Sally was a runaway,' added Emily. 'A runaway from an orphanage.' Emily peered at Sally. 'Are you?'

'Aye,' Sally replied. 'I am.'

'Sally!' I cried so loudly that the sheep in our shearing pen stared over.

'It's the truth, man Tom.'

'But it's supposed to be a secret,' I said, throwing my hands up in despair.

'I won't tell anyone,' promised Emily. 'Not for anything in the world I won't. Where was the orphanage, Sally?'

And as the cuckoo called from somewhere in the woods close to where the German airman hid, Sally told Emily her story.

'Your dad came back for you?' Emily asked.

'But they sent him away,' Sally replied.

'Cos he was a German?' Emily gasped. 'Was he really a German?'

'Why aye, a proper German. Wasn't he, Tommy?'

'Well, Auntie Annie said it was possible,' I said.

'What? You told Auntie Annie?' Sally cried. 'What else did you tell her?'

'Not much,' I said. 'Anyway, you've told Emily.'

As we stared at each other, the cuckoo's steady call suddenly wobbled.

'But how did you manage to run away from the orphanage?' Emily asked.

Sally grinned. 'Easy-peasy. I was always nicking off, but I didn't have neewhere to gan so I just had to keep coming back. You see, the kitchen window in the orphanage was broken so I could get in and out whenever I wanted — like my own private hogg hole. But I couldn't get away properly until the Germans did us a favour.'

'Germans?' I questioned.

'They brought me here,' Sally said.

'How?' asked Emily.

'By making the evacuation happen,' replied Sally. 'I'd popped oot one morning and was just having a mosey aboot doon by the river, when I saw loads of kids being marched up to the station. Never seen owt like it before. You'd think the Pied Piper was in toon. I followed them. There were even more bairns at the station. The place was chocker. You couldn't yan, tan, tethera that lot. Proper bairns, mind. Bairns with real mams and dads ready to wave them off. It was the evacuation, you see. And each one had a little suitcase or a satchel, and a gas mask. Labels tied on them an' all. I tell a lie. A few of them only had a pillowcase to carry their stuff in. But they were all waiting for trains. I worked me way doon one of them queues and was nearly at the front when a fight began. Turned oot, one of the mams didn't want them to take her bonny bairn away. She'd come to take her back home. A gadgie with a clipboard tried to stop her, but the mam knocked him doon like a skittle. Then, shrieking and screaming, she hoyed away the satchel and label, and carried her bairn away. Finders keepers, losers weepers, I picked up the satchel and label. There was a name on the label.'

'Ethel Kirkup,' I whispered.

Sally winked. 'Gan to the top of the class, bright lad. Just then the train whistle blew and our queue was told to get on board. So we did. The new Ethel Kirkup included.' Sally savoured the memory. 'The last thing I saw of Tyneside was the river, where Old Jinny had pulled us oot like a salmon.'

'Weren't you frightened?' Emily asked.

Sally shook her head. 'Never been happier. Journey took all day. Kept on stopping and back tracking, and getting oot the way of troop trains. Some of them other kids were sick, some of them boohooing fit to break their hearts. Not me. I wanted the train to gan on forever. The further we got from that orphanage, the better. We could have gone to the moon if it was up to me. At last we stopped, and everyone got off. But that wasn't it. We had to walk the rest of the way — right up into the fells. Each time we came to a village, we'd be lined up in a hall, where a load of grown-ups was waiting. If they wanted you, they took you. Didn't matter what you thought. One lass kicked and screamed — she wanted to stay with her big brother. Nobody listened to her.'

Emily shuddered.

'In the end,' Sally continued, 'I was the only one left. Usual story — neeone wanted a wild one like me. Then I saw him for the first time.'

'Scarcross?' I whispered.

'Old Smellysnake himself,' said Sally. '"She's no use," he told the evacuee committee. "I need a strong boy. Not some puny lass. I want someone to do a day's work." The evacuee committee said — take her or leave her. There weren't nee boys left.'

'So he took you?' Emily asked.

Sally laughed. 'He made us climb into the back of the cart, with the milk churns. "I'm not having you anywhere near me, you filthy toe-rag," he said, "your head's full of lice." That suited me just fine. I could just look oot and see where I was. I loved it in the fells. Right from the start. The only hills I'd ever seen were colliery spoil heaps, but these mountains seemed to reach the sky. Everything was purple. I'd never seen real heather before. "So what do they call you on Tyneside, then?" he asked when we came to the crossroads. Well, he hadn't even looked at me label, none of the committee had, so I took it off and hid it in me satchel. "Sally," I said. "Sally Smith." You see, I'd always been called Sally.'

'Why Smith?' I asked.

Sally tapped the side of her nose knowingly. 'Must be a million Smiths in the world. So how could anybody notice an extra one and send her back? Soon as I said it, I liked it. I was someone new. I was Sally Smith. Then I saw Woundale for the first time. The tarn, the trees, the woods, the cows — so bonny! And the air so fresh and clear that I thought I could drink it. I said to meself — this is where I'm supposed to be, not locked up in some coal cellar.'

'Hey, you pack of chinwaggers,' Auntie Annie said, coming over. 'Time to get back to work.'

We slowly climbed to our feet. None of us wanted to leave the shade.

'Have you noticed?' Auntie Annie asked and pointed over to the woods.

'Noticed what?' I said, exchanging a glance with Sally.

'He's changed his note. The cuckoo.'

'How do you mean, Auntie Annie?' Sally asked.

'Haven't you heard the old cuckoo rhyme?' Auntie Annie returned.

Sally shook her head.

'In April, come I will,' Auntie Annie began.

'In May, I sing all day,' Emily continued.

'In June, I change my tune,' I added.

Then, for a few moments the four of us listened to the cuckoo calling from the bulrushes. The familiar two-toned note that had chimed out over Woundale all summer sounded broken.

'You're right,' said Sally. 'It gone all trembly.'

Auntie Annie nodded. 'That means he'll be gone soon.'

4

We hadn't been back clipping for long when I saw something glinting on the road coming down into Woundale. It was the sun catching on a bicycle wheel. It could only mean one thing. Sergeant Collinson was coming.

Sally had seen it too. But instead of jumping up and running away as fast as she could, she just raised a hand to block the glare of the sun, and calmly watched the policeman wheel down into the dale.

'That's nee bobby,' she declared at last.

'You sure?' I demanded.

We watched the bike come closer.

'Sally's right,' cried Emily. 'He's not wearing a policeman's hat.'

It took a while longer before I realised who it was cycling down into Woundale. The bike belonged to somebody even worse than Sergeant Collinson. It was the angel of death. The angel of death was what everybody called the telegram boy, because he always brought bad news. The worst possible news. War Office telegrams were sent to tell families that someone was missing in action, or had been killed. We already knew that my father was missing in action. A second telegram could mean only one thing.

I looked over at my aunts. They'd seen him too. Auntie Gladys stood there with her head bowed. Auntie Dolly was weeping. Only Auntie Annie was still clipping.

Numbly I watched Auntie Annie carefully finish the yowe she was working on, then she walked over to the house to meet the telegram lad. Slowly, reluctantly, my other aunties followed.

Ever since my dad had been declared missing in action, I'd dreaded this moment. Dreaded the arrival of the telegram confirming that he would never be coming home. A large red damselfly flew towards me. It landed on my arm. I didn't move. The sun sparkled on the damselfly's brand-new, barely-dried wings. It had just emerged from the tarn. The next thing I knew, my name was being shouted by my aunties. They weren't just shouting, they were yelling. My name echoed across Woundale loud as a hundred cuckoos.

'You're wanted,' Sally murmured.

Looking up, I could see my aunties running towards me. The damselfly darted away. Fear of what I was about to hear clawed through me like a rat in a heap of fodder beet.

'Remember the rainbow,' Sally whispered. 'My dad, your dad — they're both going to be all right.'

Something inside of me broke at these words. 'He's dead, Sally,' I stuttered. 'Don't you understand? My dad's dead.'

'No, he's not, Tommy.'

'You're always saying that,' I cried. 'But you're wrong.' 'You'll see—'

'You're just making it worse.' My words rose on a sob. 'Leave me alone.'

My eyes were so full of tears that I could barely see the telegram Auntie Annie was waving.

'Tommy!' Auntie Annie cried.

I felt her throw her arms round me.

'Tommy!' she cried again. 'Tommy!'

But there was something strange in the tone of her voice. She didn't sound as though she were bringing bad news. In fact, the opposite. She sounded — elated.

'He's alive!' she burst.

All at once Auntie Gladys and Auntie Dolly were hugging and kissing me, telling me what had happened to my father. How his plane had been hit somewhere over Holland. How he'd managed to parachute out. How some Dutch children had found him and hidden him from the Nazis on their farm. How he had made his way back to England through the secret underground network. And that he couldn't wait to see us all again.

'There's a letter as well as a telegram,' Auntie Gladys explained. 'The War Office have sent it on. He'll be back soon. Just think of that!' Auntie Gladys grinned. 'Our Arthur will be back in Woundale soon.'

But I couldn't take it in. All I could do was laugh. We

were all laughing. Dancing too. My aunties and Vi and even the telegram boy. He kept singing: 'For he's a jolly good fellow!' and saying over and over: 'I never get to give good news like this.'

Seeing the celebration, the Hawkrigg brothers came over. Soon followed by everyone else. They all wanted to know the good news.

'We've got to have a party,' Auntie Annie declared. 'Dolly, put the kettle on!'

We all cheered.

'I'm going to open a jar of my best strawberry jam as well,' Auntie Annie added. 'And Mr Rebanks brought us a jar of his honey this morning.'

'I'll make some honey biscuits,' Auntie Gladys said.

'Let's have a tea party!' cried Auntie Dolly.

With a grin, Auntie Annie plucked off her headscarf and flung it high in the air: 'We're having a party, and everyone's invited,' she shouted. 'Leave them sheep be for an hour.'

We all cheered again. I looked round for Sally.

But Sally was nowhere to be seen. Where was she? I sprinted away from the sheep pens. Had she gone to the giant's parlour? I had to find her and tell her that everything really was going to be all right. This was the perfect time for us to tell Auntie Annie about the airman. Now that she knew my dad had been saved by some other farm children, she'd understand why we'd helped the Woundale airman. She'd be able to sort everything out.

Reaching the woods, I rushed through the trees and was passing under the old oak when I heard her. She was perched up in the branches where we'd found the airman, and for the first time since I'd known her, she was crying. She was definitely crying. That soft sound wasn't the murmur of the breeze through the oak leaves, it was Sally weeping.

'What's the matter, Sal?'

'Nothing.'

'Didn't you hear — my dad's alive. He's really alive!'

'I'm so glad for you,' she said through her tears. 'Honest. Me heart feels like one of them skylarks up on the fells. The way they fly higher and higher until they touch heaven.' She sniffed.

'Come down, we're having a party. Tea. Strawberry jam too. And Auntie Gladys is making honey biscuits.'

'A tea party,' Sally said in the smallest voice I had ever heard her use. 'How lovely.'

'And you're invited.'

It was horrible hearing her so upset.

'Maybe it'll come good for you as well,' I said, desperately.

'How do you mean, Tom?'

'Maybe your dad will come back for you again.'

'Do you really think so?' she asked.

'Maybe. After the war.'

All at once, she was her old self again. With a shout of laughter, she jumped from the tree. I only just managed to get out of the way.

Still laughing, she leapt to her feet.

'Come on,' I urged. 'Let's get back to the tea party.'

'I'll meet you there,' she said. 'Got something to do first.'

'What?'

Her answer was to dart away into the trees. I ran after her. She soon slipped from view, but I could hear her up ahead for a little while. Then all I could hear was the cuckoo's cracked note. Was it the cuckoo calling or was it Sally whistling through her teeth?

I followed the sound until I found myself in the woods behind the Scarcross place. Down below was Sally's byre and the back of Scarcross's grey house. I could see his kitchen garden. I could see Sally too. She had one of Scarcross's wicker trug baskets and was filling it with his prized strawberries.

When the trug was full, she hurried over.

'For the party,' she said, holding up the strawberries.

'And what if Scarcross is there, and sees you bringing them?'

'He won't,' she replied. 'They're for the Alleyman.'

'The Alleyman?'

'Why aye, Tom. Why can't he have a party as well? Mebbees he's like your dad. Mebbees, he's got a bairn waiting for him to come home. A lad like you. Or,' Sally paused for a moment. 'A lass like me. Tommy, don't you see how right we've been to help him? The Dutch kids helped your dad, and we've helped the Alleyman. We were meant to. Just like they were meant to help your dad.'

'That's why Auntie Annie will understand.'

'Understand what?'

'When we tell her what we've been doing.'

But Sally wasn't listening. 'Besides, he's going to be canny thirsty on a day like this. Nowt like strawbs for a hot day.'

And with that, she hurried away through the woods. At the Giant's Teeth, she pulled aside the 'front door', then disappeared down the tunnel. Fighting back the fear I always felt when going near the German airman, I crawled in after her. This is the last time, I promised myself.

'Just me and Tommy,' Sally was calling. 'Got you a real treat, Alleyman.'

My heart thrashed against my ribs like a brown trout thrown onto a beck bank. I couldn't forget that he was an enemy soldier, even if Sally had.

The moment I got into the den, I was shocked to find the airman sitting up. He looked far more alert than yesterday. He was smiling too. His grogginess and shivering seemed to have gone.

'*Danke,*' he said. '*Danke, Kinder.*'

'He's thanking us for being kind,' said Sally. 'Nee bother, Alleyman. We're happy to help.'

'*Tausend Dank.*'

'A thousand thanks,' Sally translated. 'Nee bother, Mr Alleyman.'

Suddenly the airman stretched out his arm. I pulled back. But he continued to hold his hand out and grinned.

'He just wants to shake hands,' Sally said.

The German nodded. '*Handschlag.*'

'Handshake,' explained Sally, and shook his hand.

'*Ja, ja,*' said the airman. '*Handschlag mit dem Jungen.*'

'Handshake with them young'uns,' Sally said. 'Go on then, Tommy, he wants to shake your hand.'

Shake his hand? This was too much. I shook my head instead. How can you shake hands with an enemy? The airman seemed to understand and dropped his arm.

'That's not very nice,' said Sally. 'I bet your dad shook hands with those Dutch bairns.'

'But they're not the enemy.'

'I thought we all helped each other in Woundale.'

Before I realised what I was doing, I put my hand out. The German airman shook it.

'*Tausend Dank.*'

'And a thousand strawberries. We brought this for you,' Sally grinned, and held out the trug.

As Sally and the airman were wolfing down the strawberries, I noticed that there was a fresh bandage round the airman's head. A shadow of dark bristles had grown on his cheeks. The food Sally had left had gone. But both bottles were still full of water, and wet on the outside. I reached out and touched them.

Then I realised something else. Those bottles had just been filled. They were ice cold. The airman must be strong enough to have found the beck for himself.

Sally was sitting right beside him now. 'Look,' she said, pointing to her teeth. 'Me and you have both got a gap.' Biting a strawberry in two, she showed him the teeth marks. 'See?'

The airman laughed and pointed to his own teeth. '*Lücke.*'

'Yes we are lucky,' Sally beamed. 'Have another strawb, Mr Alleyman.'

They were still eating when I heard the sound of someone crawling up the tunnel. My first instinct was to run. But there was nowhere to go. Like a rabbit caught in a snare, I waited. Sally looked at me. Then she looked at the airman. The airman's hand darted to his coverall pocket, and reached inside. He drew out a Luger pistol. Whoever it was, was getting closer. There was a sharp click as the airman cocked his weapon. Sally's eyes widened.

5

'Emily!' Sally cried when her bright blonde hair came into view.

'I saw you. I was following you,' Emily explained, out of breath. 'But I lost you. Then I heard your voices. Is this your den?'

Before I could stop her, Emily had squeezed past me. When she saw the German airman with his gun, she let out a short, sharp shriek. Eyes darting, the airman stared at each of us in turn. Then still as a hunting heron, he listened intently. He was trying to hear into the woods beyond the giant's parlour. *'Soldaten?'* he whispered.

My head swirled. But Sally didn't seem frightened at all. 'Nee soldiers,' she told him. 'Just Emily. You don't need to worry about her. She won't tell anyone you're here, will you, Emily?'

'Never,' Emily whispered fervently, eyes growing wider and wider as she stared at the airman. 'So there is a German,' she said. 'And he's in Woundale.'

The airman listened keenly for a bit longer. He must have

realised that no soldiers were coming because he sighed and put the gun back in his coverall pocket. Reaching for the strawberries, he took a handful.

'Got something to tell you as well,' Sally was saying to the airman. 'You'll never guess. My dad's an Alleyman just like you. A sailor.'

As Sally continued talking, all I could do was stare at the bulge in his coverall pocket. Now I knew — he did have a Luftwaffe Luger pistol.

'So turns out I was right to help you, wasn't I, Mr Alleyman?' Sally carried on, munching on a strawberry herself and passing the trug to Emily. 'Cos I'm a Jerry too. Well, at least half of one. I'm Sally the Alleyman.'

The airman crammed another strawberry into his mouth, then reached inside his other pocket. He pulled out a photograph. '*Mein Baby*,' the airman said, handing the picture to Sally.

'It's his baby,' Sally murmured.

'*Meine Tochter*,' the German added.

'His doctor?' Emily asked.

'His daughter,' whispered Sally, gazing at the photograph. 'It's him holding his baby girl.'

For a while, Sally just gazed at the picture. Emily stared at the German airman as she slowly chewed a strawberry. The airman peered at each of us in turn.

'We'd better go now,' I said at last. 'The tea party, remember? Auntie Annie will be wondering where we are.'

Sally handed the photograph back. The German kissed it then put it in his pocket.

'I'll leave the strawbs here for you,' Sally said. 'And we'll come back later. Scran as many as you like. There's more where that little lot came from.'

We crawled back down the tunnel. Sally carefully put the front door back in place. I ran ahead. Despite everything, I felt a wave of relief rush over me. Now Emily knew about the German airman, it was only a matter of time before everyone did. Two people might be able to carry a secret, but three never can — one of them will always drop it. It was time to tell Auntie Annie everything. No matter what Sally said. This time she wouldn't talk me round. And I wasn't breaking any promises either. The moment Emily found us all in the giant's parlour, the promise had been broken.

'Wait,' Sally called after me. 'You've got to be a witness.'

'I'm telling Auntie Annie everything,' I said.

But Sally wasn't listening. She was holding Tilly. 'I've been telling Emily how we have to swear on Tilly to keep the secret of our Alleyman airman. Here, Emily, take Tilly. We'll make the promise now. Hold her up high.'

Emily did as she was told.

'Repeat after me,' Sally began. 'I, Emily Rebanks . . .'

'I, Emily Rebanks . . .' Emily replied.

'Do solemnly swear . . .'

'There's no point,' I blurted.

'Course there is,' Sally retorted. 'She has to promise on Tilly.'

'Sally, we're going to tell Auntie Annie about the German airman.'

'Not this again, Tommy man.'

'She'll find out anyway, now that Emily knows.'

'Divvent you trust neebody?'

'I don't think she'll tell on purpose,' I said.

'I won't tell anyone,' said Emily.

'It'll just happen,' I explained. 'Maybe not tonight, maybe not tomorrow, but the day after.'

Sally grinned. 'So, why not let him be, until then? Tell Auntie Annie tomorrow. What's the matter with you, Tommy? Is your dad the only one that's allowed to be safe?'

'How can he be safe here?' I demanded. 'Scarcross could find him at any time. And what about you? You're already in enough trouble with Sergeant Collinson without harbouring an enemy. Auntie Annie will know what to do. If we don't tell her, they'll take you away. Sergeant Collinson is rounding up all the runaways. There's a place where they're all being taken. An institution. Is that what you want?'

Without me realising, I had begun to shout. Sally stared at me. I stared back. Neither of us blinked. It was Emily who broke the silence. 'Maybe that's why he came here,' she said.

'Why who came here?' I demanded.

'The German airman,' said Emily. 'Maybe he's come for Sally.'

'What are you talking about?' I cried.

'What do you mean, Emily?' Sally asked at the same time.

'Maybe he knows your dad,' said Emily. 'They're both Germans, aren't they? Well, maybe he's come to take you back to him.'

'Balderdash,' I said, no longer shouting, but even more frustrated.

'Or maybe,' said Emily. 'He *is* your dad. He looks like you, Sally. I mean, that gap between his teeth.'

Sally looked like someone who'd been struck by lightning — and was still alive. 'Do you really think I look like him?' she whispered.

'Yes. He must be your dad,' said Emily. 'He came on a boat the first time and now he's come in a plane. Why else would he show you that photograph? It must be a picture of you when you were a baby. He's come to take you home.'

'Take her home?' I cried. 'More like he's a spy sending out signals for the invasion.'

'He's not like that,' said Sally. 'He's a good enemy.'

'What about his gun?' I burst.

'All soldiers have a gun,' Sally retorted. 'He wouldn't hurt us.'

'When Emily came in, he was ready to shoot her.'

'Only because he thought she was soldiers.'

'And he could easily shoot any of us.'

'Well, why hasn't he? He's had enough chances!' Sally exclaimed. 'Please, divvent tell,' she begged.

'I have to,' I said. 'I'm going to.'

And I walked on ahead without looking back. I knew that my dad would think the same: it was time to tell the truth.

6

Back at the house, it really was like a party. The lovely sweet smell of baking honey biscuits filled the kitchen. Everybody, even the telegram boy, was gathered. Vi was jumping up and down. Everyone was laughing.

'There you are, Tommy,' Auntie Annie greeted me. 'Where've you been? You're just in time. The honey biscuits are ready.'

'Where's Sally?' Auntie Gladys asked, handing me a biscuit. Before I could reply, Emily came into the kitchen.

'Hello, pet,' Auntie Dolly greeted her. 'Sally with you?'

'She's popped upstairs,' Emily replied. 'To get Vi a ribbon for her hair.'

The biscuit warm in my hand, I took a deep breath. There was no easy way. I was just going to have to tell Auntie Annie as best I could. I couldn't waste any more time. 'Auntie Annie,' I announced. 'I need to talk to you.'

She must have realised that I had something important to say because she said: 'Dolly, see everyone's got plenty of tea. Tommy and I are popping outside for a minute.'

But before Auntie Annie could open the door, someone began knocking at it. Sergeant Collinson stood on the doorstep.

'Hello, Miss Grisedale,' he said.

'Sergeant Collinson,' Auntie Annie answered.

For a moment, I just stood there, staring at the bushy moustache that curved over Sergeant Collinson's top lip like a fox's tail.

'I hear you've had a bit of good news,' he said.

'A bit?' Auntie Annie laughed. 'Our Arthur's safe and sound. We're having a party. Come in, there's tea and biscuits all round.'

'I won't if you don't mind. I'm afraid I'm here on official business. I'm sorry to interfere with the Woundale Clipping and your good news, but needs must.'

Auntie Annie nodded. 'I've an idea what's brought you here, but let me tell you before you begin, that Bertie Tupperman got what he was asking for. And Miss Gently's a fool. As for what Mr Scarcross has been saying—'

'I'm not here about any of that,' Sergeant Collinson interrupted.

'Well, what are you here for then?' Auntie Annie demanded.

'Turns out, the little evacuee lass is on the register.'

'Register?'

'The runaway register,' replied Sergeant Collinson. 'She's absconded from an orphanage asylum on Tyneside. And I'm afraid I have orders to apprehend her.'

'Apprehend her?' Auntie Annie retorted. 'Anyone would think she was a criminal. You ought to be ashamed of yourself, a great big man like you, coming after a slip of a bairn like her.'

The policeman stroked his foxtail moustache uneasily. 'Truth be told, I don't like it any more than you do.'

'Don't do it then,' returned Auntie Annie sharply.

'Orders from above, Miss Grisedale. Is Mr Scarcross within your premises? I need to talk to him, since she's his evacuee.'

'Mr Scarcross?' Auntie Annie cried. 'Yes, that's who you should be talking to — with a pair of handcuffs at the ready to arrest him. He's not fit to have an evacuee. And as for the way he treats Simon. Well, that poor lad's found his voice now, and you should hear what he says. Scarcross practically drowned him, as well as half-starving him. Oh, I could tell you any number of things that that man has done. And I'm not even going to mention cruelty to animals. He threw a hammer at our Tommy and Sally. And then fired his shotgun inches from Sally.'

'Wilfully discharging his firearm in the close presence of children?' Sergeant Collinson asked.

'And that's just the start.'

The policeman nodded. 'Aye, it's time we dealt with that one. I've heard others say things about Mr Scarcross. But first things first. It's the lass I want now. Orders are orders, Annie. There's nothing you or I can do. It's out of my hands.'

Auntie Annie sighed. 'Tommy,' she told me. 'Go and fetch Sally. And we'll see if we can't clear this whole thing up.'

'Happen it's gone beyond that I'm afraid,' said Sergeant Collinson.

I went back to the tea party. My only hope had been Auntie Annie, now it seemed there was nothing she could do either. And when they found out about the airman, then they might send Sally to prison, let alone to the special institution Scarcross had mentioned.

'Is Sally still upstairs?' I asked Emily.

'She's gone,' Emily whispered.

'Gone?'

Emily nodded. 'She's run away. She didn't go upstairs. She never even came into the house. I had to promise not to follow her. And to give you a message. She said you'd understand. She said, "Tell Tommy, everything's going to be all right now. The rainbow said so." The rainbow said so, what does that mean?'

'I don't know,' I said.

And I really didn't. I didn't know anything any more. All I knew was that Sally had run off and the only thing I could do for her now was buy her some time so she could get safely away. I'd probably never see her again. The happiest day had become the saddest.

'Well, lad?' Sergeant Collinson asked from the door. 'Have you got the little evacuee lassie?'

'She's not here,' I heard myself say. 'She's still playing outside. In the woods.'

'Well go and fetch her,' Auntie Annie snapped.

Pretending to be in a hurry, I ran round the tarn. But when I came into the woods, I sat under the old oak. What had she said about the first rule of playing the wag? Gan as far as you can, quick as you can. She'd have left Woundale already.

And Sally wasn't the only one who'd gone. As I sat beneath the airman's tree, I realised that I couldn't hear the cuckoo calling. He'd started his own long journey back to Africa. I lay on my back and stared up at the tree. Now I knew how a riggweltered sheep felt.

I stayed for as long as I dared then headed back home. At least now she had a head start.

Auntie Annie and Sergeant Collinson weren't the only ones waiting for me when I got back to the house. Scarcross was there. He stared at me like a snake waiting to strike.

'Well then, Thomas?' Sergeant Collinson asked, mopping his brow with a handkerchief. 'Where is she?'

'I can't find her,' I said. 'I've looked everywhere.'

'I knew it,' growled Scarcross. 'She's bolted. Heard the law was after her, so she's slung her hook. Flitted. That's what runaways do — they spend their lives doing off.'

'Have you any idea at all where she might be, Thomas?' Sergeant Collinson asked.

I shook my head, glad to be able to tell the truth.

'I'll turn the Home Guard out,' said Scarcross. 'We'll soon track her down.'

'There's no need for that,' Auntie Annie said.

'No need?' Scarcross demanded. 'I should think there's every need. On top of everything else, she broke into my house last night and vandalised the place. Smashed my best table and shattered a valuable tea set. She's nicked me torch an' all — that's army equipment.'

'Broke into your house?' put in Sergeant Collinson. 'I thought she was your evacuee. Doesn't she live with you?'

'He has her in the byre,' said Auntie Annie.

'What, with the beasts?' Sergeant Collinson said.

'Animals should live with animals,' said Scarcross.

Sergeant Collinson glared at Scarcross. 'Seems you've abdicated your responsibility with that evacuee. So I'll deal with Miss Grisedale on the matter.'

'Sergeant Collinson,' Auntie Annie said. 'I'll find her. If it takes me all day and all night, I'll find her and bring her into town.'

Sergeant Collinson fingered his foxtail moustache. 'Well, strictly speaking I should bring her in now, but since you've a celebration and the clipping going on, I'll let you bring her to town tomorrow morning. I'll leave her for tonight. First thing tomorrow morning, mind. I'm trusting you.'

'She'll be there,' replied Auntie Annie.

'That's no good,' snapped Scarcross. 'She wants bringing in now. The Home Guard will—'

'This is a police matter, Mr Scarcross,' Sergeant Collinson interrupted. 'And I'd thank you to mind your own business. Tomorrow morning, Annie.'

We watched Sergeant Collinson push his bike up the road out of Woundale.

Scarcross spat dismissively. 'You'll never find her. She's got more tricks than a bag of weasels. Pal of mine has a team of hounds. What we need to do is give the dogs her scent and they'll sharp run her down. I'll have to look in the byre for something.'

'You heard what Sergeant Collinson said,' Auntie Annie retorted. 'It's a police matter.'

'Oh, that idiot Collinson will soon come begging me to find her. I'll get my sheep finished then I'll soon run her to ground in the morning. A night on the fells will do her good.' And with that, he went back to his sheep.

7

'Things have gone too far, haven't they?' Auntie Annie began as she closed the door behind us.

I nodded wretchedly. Scarcross was right. Sergeant Collinson might not be able to find her, but the hounds would. They could chase a fox over twenty miles of fell, and when they caught the fox, they always killed it. In my mind I could already hear Scarcross and his hounds chasing Sally down, and there was nothing I could do to help her.

'If you know where she is,' Auntie Annie was saying, 'you must tell me. You aren't helping her by telling lies. Do the pair of you have a special den or some place where she might go to hide?'

All at once, I realised that maybe I did know where she was. How could I have been so stupid?

'She might be hiding with the German airman!' I cried.

Auntie Annie gaped at me as though I was speaking a foreign language. 'German airman? Talk sense, Tommy.'

'He's been in Woundale all this time,' I explained. 'He parachuted down from the plane and we've been hiding him.'

'I've never heard such a tall tale in all my born days.'

'It's true, Auntie Annie,' I insisted desperately. 'He was badly injured and all shivery. Sally put a bandage round his head. Gave him food and medicine. And she said she was running away, but I think she might be hiding in the giant's parlour with him.'

'Giant's parlour?'

'It's what we call our den at the Giant's Teeth.'

Auntie Annie stared at me open mouthed.

'You see, Sally trusts him,' I went on. 'And she shouldn't. He seems kind and he thanked us. But he's a Jerry. And she'll trust him even more now that Emily's told her he's her dad. You see, I think Sally really believes it. They've both got a gap between their front teeth—'

'That's enough!' Auntie Annie warned. 'I don't want to hear any more. You know exactly where she is, Tommy. I just don't understand what's got into you. Your dad would be ashamed of you, Thomas.'

The words were like a blow. 'No,' I shot back. 'He'd be proud of me, because we've been helping the airman just like those Dutch farm children helped him. Not so he can escape, but so that he can surrender safely. We had to stop Scarcross shooting him.'

'You really expect me to believe that Sally is hiding with a German airman?'

'It's true, Auntie Annie. And he's got a gun.'

Auntie Annie took a deep breath. 'You've got carried away,

our Tommy. I know young Sally has got a good imagination, and Gladys and Dolly have put their two penn'orth in about there being a German airman in Woundale. And what with your dad being missing. Maybe it's my fault an' all. I haven't kept as close an eye on you as I should.' She sighed. 'Well, since you won't tell me where she is, I'll go and look myself.'

'I'll take you to her, Auntie Annie,' I begged. 'Then you'll see him for yourself.'

Auntie Annie stared hard at me.

'You're really telling me that Sally is with a German airman?'

At that moment the house door opened and we could hear the sounds of the party. The telegram boy was singing: 'Wish Me Luck as You Wave Me Goodbye'.

'What are you two up to?' Auntie Gladys asked. 'Come and see Vi dancing. Forget the sheep for a minute. What's the matter, our Annie?'

It was as Auntie Gladys stood there staring at us that Auntie Annie made up her mind. I could see that she'd decided to believe me.

'Gladys,' she said. 'The German airman's in Woundale.'

'What?' Auntie Gladys cried.

'And he's got our Sally. You stay here. Tommy come with me.'

Before Auntie Gladys could react, Auntie Annie was running towards the woods. I'd never seen her move so fast. In no time at all, we'd reached the stone circle. I pulled the 'front door' branches away, and Auntie Annie darted down the tunnel.

'Stop,' I gasped. 'He's got a Luftwaffe Luger.'

She didn't stop. I plunged in after her.

'There's no one here,' Auntie Annie said quietly when I reached her.

She was right, the giant's parlour was empty.

'I can see you've been having a picnic,' Auntie Annie said, pointing at the trug which was full of strawberry hulls.

'He's gone,' I said.

'Is this another one of your lies, Thomas?' Auntie Annie asked coldly.

'He's been living here since he cut himself down from the tree,' I explained. 'We kept spare food for him in the larder. There was a first aid kit, and he used his parachute for a pillow.'

But even as I spoke, I realised that everything had vanished. Then I noticed that the pile of branches concealing the larder was more than twice its usual size. I crawled past Auntie Annie and started digging into the heap.

'This has gone far enough,' Auntie Annie snapped.

'Wait,' I cried, and burying through a layer of twigs and leaves I pulled out the folded parachute.

Auntie Annie took it from me and carefully unfolded it, then rolled it up again. 'It's a parachute,' she agreed quietly. 'Oh, Tommy, you were telling the truth.' Her face froze. 'So where's Sally? He must have taken her hostage.'

8

Parachute under her arm, Auntie Annie hurried out of the woods. Before we reached the farm, she suddenly stopped. 'I don't care what you and Sally have been doing, Tommy,' she said, 'all I want is for you to go to town as quickly as you ever can. I'll send the shepherds along behind you as soon as I've told them exactly what's going on. But you go now. When you get there, tell Sergeant Collinson that the German airman has been hiding in Woundale and he's got Sally. Tell him we need proper soldiers here. Do you understand?'

I'd only taken a few paces when she called after me.

'I'll find that lass, if it's the last thing I do. I'll bring her home safe and sound.'

But I could tell that Auntie Annie was scared.

'Get your bike and keep to the road,' she finished. 'The shepherds will come after you. Now go!'

Auntie Annie had already gone back into the house so I didn't have to explain that I'd left my bike under the bridge.

I was soon up on the fells. The skylarks rose as high as

ever and the bog cotton danced in the wind. Yet everything else was different. Maybe Sally would never get to taste the bilberries whose bushes marched up the mountains. I forced myself to run as fast as I could until my breath tore from my lungs. Once I'd got my bike, I'd be able to reach town before the shepherds caught up with me. We needed the regular army out as soon as possible.

Even though I was up on the tops, it was hotter than ever — the kind of muggy weather that makes you sweat even when you're just walking. I glanced up. Clouds were building in the sky.

At last the humpback bridge came into view. I scurried down under its stone arch. Nothing could have prepared me for what I found there.

'Areet, bonny lad, what's the matter with you? You look as though you've seen a ghost.'

'Sally,' I stammered, barely able to talk. 'What are you doing?'

'Can't you see?' she returned. 'I'm making a daisy chain.'

She was grinning happily. Then I saw them — the long black boots. Behind Sally, the German airman was lying in the alders.

'He'll be all right in a minute,' she announced. 'He's conked oot. We only just managed to get this far. He's not as strong as I thought he was. We're waiting here until he can carry on.'

'Auntie Annie knows,' I gasped, 'everything.'

But Sally kept on making her daisy chain. 'You see, he needed to run away an' all,' she said. 'Kept saying *Wasser, Wasser* and *Boot, Boot*. Until I worked out that he meant boat. He wanted to know the way to where boats gan on the water. He wanted to know the way to the sea. So, I thought I might as well show him.'

'Sally,' I repeated. 'Auntie Annie knows.'

'And lucky I did,' Sally continued. 'Thing is, he didn't know how to get oot of Woundale without being seen. So I showed him the back door.'

'You climbed up the force?'

'Why aye. That's why I told Emily to tell you about the rainbow. Hoped you'd follow us. We nearly fell doon, mind. He was proper dizzy. When we reached the top, he had to lean on me. He's canny heavy.' Sally looked up from the daisy chain. 'There wasn't a rainbow there today, Tom. But it doesn't matter, does it? Cos there was one there the other day. And we've both got our lucky gap.'

'Everyone's looking for you.'

'I'm glad you've found us, Tommy,' she said. 'You see, we need your help to get to the sea.'

'Listen, Sally, I've been sent to town to tell Sergeant Collinson.'

'Tell him what?'

'To get the army out.'

Sally sighed. 'Do you really want them to shoot him?'

'They won't.'

'Somehow Scarcross will get him.'

'That's why I've been sent to town, to get the proper army.'

'They'll probably just shoot him an' all. All they know is that he's a Jerry. They don't know him like we do. Neeone does. And they'll dee something else. They'll lock me up for good.'

I didn't reply. What could I say? Besides, I had run out of words. The truth was, ever since the airman had landed in Woundale, Sally and I had fallen feet first into an adventure. And like a pair of sticks thrown into a fast-running beck, now I was just going to have to see where it carried us. I sat there under the bridge, as the airman lay in the alders, and Sally's daisy chain got longer and longer.

The airman groaned, but he didn't stir.

'Whisht, gadgies coming,' Sally suddenly whispered.

There were voices in the distance. Footsteps on the road.

'Someone's coming from Woundale,' Sally said.

'It'll be the shepherds,' I replied. 'Auntie Annie said—'

'Haad your gob.' Sally pressed a finger to her lips. The voices and footsteps grew louder, then stopped on the bridge directly above us.

'Give us a fag then,' one of them ordered.

'Scarecross,' Sally mouthed.

We heard a match strike, then the stench of cigarette smoke reached us on the wind. 'Now, don't forget,' Scarcross said. 'All you two have to do is fetch the hounds. Leave the rest to me.'

'But Miss Grisedale said we had to catch up with Tommy and tell Sergeant Collinson,' one of the shepherds said.

'What does she know about Jerries?' Scarcross interrupted. 'This is a matter for me and my pals in the Home Guard now.'

'Don't you think we should leave it to the regular army?' the other shepherd argued.

'No, I chuffing well don't,' thundered Scarcross. 'You think I spent four years fighting that lot, just to let one of them wander about in my own back yard?'

'Sounds like you're looking for revenge,' said the first shepherd.

'Too right I am. It's an eye for an eye. And if anyone knows what that means, I do, because they took one from me.'

The footsteps started again. The stink of cigarette smoke faded. Sally darted up and peered over the edge of the bridge.

'He's got his gun,' she whispered. 'A shepherd on either side of him.'

She hurried back down.

'We'd best flit, Tommy. Help me wake him, and get him onto his feet.'

'You'll never get there,' I said, half to myself. 'Never get to the sea.'

Sally began to chuckle. 'I haven't told you everything, Tommy man. Do you want me to?'

I didn't reply.

'I'm gannin' with him,' Sally said. 'Not just to the sea, but to Germany.'

Nothing she said or did could have surprised me now.

'Aye,' she grinned. 'We're gannin' to Germany together. You see, Emily was right. He is my dad. That's why he's here. He became a navigator so he could find me. Then he parachuted doon into Woundale just for me. He wants me to gan with him.'

Gently I shook my head.

'I'm going home with my dad,' said Sally, eyes shining.

Suddenly, the airman stirred. Groaning, he sat up. He was paler than ever. Fresh blood had soaked through his bandage.

'Sally,' he said. Then he saw me. 'Tommy. *Alles gut?*' the airman asked, watching us closely.

Sally nodded. 'Aye, all is good.' She turned to me and giggled. 'See, I can even speak Alleyman.' Then she turned back to the airman. 'Tommy's come to help. Now howay, up you get. We won't get to the sea just lying here.'

Grinding his teeth, the airman stood up.

'Howay, Tom,' Sally whispered to me. 'You'll do this last thing for me, won't you? We've got to gan before Scarcross comes back.'

She stood there looking at me pleadingly. Somehow, we managed to hoist the airman back up onto the road.

'We'll be your crutches,' Sally told him.

The airman flung a limp arm round my shoulder. My knees almost buckled under his weight.

With Sally and me on either side, we staggered our way towards the crossroads. It was getting dark. When I looked up, I saw the clouds had turned black. A storm was gathering.

The stink of sweat and iodine wafting from the airman almost made me retch. I'd never been this close to him.

'Come on,' Sally urged. 'One step at a time.'

9

We'd stumbled our way to the crossroads when the rain came. I felt one fat drop, followed by another. And then the heavens opened. Within seconds we were soaked to the skin. Seeing the four ways sign, the airman grabbed hold of the post, and panting heavily, scanned the fells.

One more time, I told myself, try one more time to persuade her. 'Please, Sally,' I begged, having to shout over the din of the rain pelting the crossroads. 'It's not too late. Let's hand him in to the army. Then he'll be safe. And we won't be in any trouble. You'll be a hero for bringing in the airman. Auntie Annie won't let on that we've been hiding him, and she'll make them let you stay in Woundale.'

Water streamed down Sally's face. Her long black hair was bedraggled. It hung over her eyes like rats' tails. 'I don't want to be a hero,' she yelled. 'I want to be with my dad.' Then she turned to the airman and pointed up at the signs. 'Take no notice of them,' she said. 'This is the way to the sea.'

Grunting, the airman let go of the signpost. He tottered

a few dizzy steps forward and leant even more heavily against us.

For me, the adventure had come to an end. I couldn't go any further. Stopping, I jerked myself out from under the airman. For a moment I thought he would fall, but Sally managed to steady him and they shuffled along through the downpour together.

'This way, to the sea,' Sally shouted, as the rain lashed yet harder. Then she turned and shouted something at me, but the hammering rain drowned out her words.

'What did you say?' I bellowed.

Her words reached me only in snatches. 'Goodbye . . . will miss you . . . tell Auntie Annie . . . never forget . . . Woundale . . .'

'You'll never get there,' I yelled after them. 'The hounds will chase you down. You'll both get shot.'

'Not us,' she yelled over her shoulder. 'Both. Born. Lucky.'

Helplessly, I watched them as they stumbled onwards. 'Come back,' I whispered.

Even if I'd screamed, she wouldn't have heard me. A strike of lightning lit up the torrential rain. I waited for the thunderclap. But it wasn't lightning. It was the beam from a vehicle. An army truck was coming from town.

The German airman must have seen it too, because suddenly he got a burst of energy and ran off the road onto the fell. Sally ran after him.

Turning heavily at the crossroads, the truck headed

towards us. I watched the airman run raggedly through the bilberry bushes. But another vehicle had stopped before the crossroads, and armed men were jumping down from it. In the teeming rain I recognised Scarcross and his pals from the Home Guard. They were running over the fellside to cut off the airman.

'That's him!' Scarcross's voice thundered. 'Shoot to kill.'

The soldiers in the truck had got out too. I could see their uniforms. They were the proper army. Now they were also sprinting through the rain towards Sally and the German airman.

Changing direction, the airman stumbled. Sally helped him catch his balance.

'Get down!' one of the proper soldiers shouted at me.

I threw myself down and buried my face into the soaking bog cotton. The last thing I saw was the airman thrusting Sally down out of danger and holding his arms up in surrender.

'Fire!' Scarcross's order resounded through the storm.

A single shotgun obeyed.

April 1941. Woundale, the Lake District, England

Epilogue

It was Sally who heard it first. She came sprinting down through the trees to tell me. 'Tommy! Tommy!' she cried. 'You'll never guess what.'

Then I heard it too. 'Cuckoo's back.' I grinned.

She laughed. 'Howay, let's gan and tell the others.'

We ran round the tarn where the daffodils were in full, golden bloom. Arnold neighed happily from his field.

'Cuckoo!' Simon called, as we hurtled past him. He was gathering water snails for his new gaggle of geese. After Scarcross was arrested, Simon had taken on the lease to the farm — and it was thriving.

We met Auntie Gladys and Auntie Dolly on our farmyard. Vi came skipping over to Sally. 'Cuckoo's back,' Auntie Gladys and Auntie Dolly said at the same time.

Auntie Annie was waiting for us at the door. 'I've heard him.' She smiled. 'April, come I will.'

'You were right, Auntie Annie,' said Sally. 'What you told me last year, when they captured the Alleyman. You said that by the time the cuckoo came back, everything would be right as rain. And it is.'

'Yes, lass, it really is, because the postman's just been,' announced Auntie Annie. 'He brought us this.'

'Has it arrived?' asked Sally, taking the envelope from Auntie Annie. She opened it, and brought out a document. 'So, is this it? Is it real?' Sally breathed.

'All legal and binding,' declared Auntie Annie.

'Oh, thank you, Auntie Annie. Thank you. I've always wanted a family more than a queen wants gold,' Sally said, as she gazed at her adoption papers.

'Well, now you've got one,' Auntie Annie laughed.

'So, you're not my Auntie Annie any more?'

Auntie Annie shook her head. 'No, I'm your mam. But there's no need to thank me. Truth is, I've always wanted a daughter of my own.'

'And now you've got one,' laughed Sally. 'And doesn't that make Tommy my brother? Because you're like a mam to him as well.'

And they hugged.

'Now off you both go and play,' whispered Auntie Annie, trying to hide the tear she was wiping away.

'Can I, Mam — even though there's a war on?'

'Yes, you can, pet. Then will you and Tommy help Simon with his new calves? He can't wait to show them to Tommy's dad when we comes home on leave next week.'

We ran back round the tarn. Reaching the old oak, Sally suddenly stopped and looked thoughtfully up into the branches.

'I did think that Alleyman was my dad, you know, Tommy,' she said. 'Well, I really wanted him to be. I'm so glad Scarcross didn't kill him when he shot him. I hope they're allowed strawberries in his Prisoner of War camp. Remember how quickly he scoffed them?'

And at that moment the cuckoo called. It was deep within the canopy above us.

'Areet,' Sally called up. 'Divvent gan on. We can hear you!' Her eyes sparked. 'By the way, bonny lad, you know what I was saying aboot Miss Gently? Well, I've got a plan, haven't I? Just wait till you hear it. You'll split your sides. And she'll never know we did it. It's the best plan I've ever had.'

And as the cuckoo called again, I listened to Sally's plan. Soon we were both helpless with laughter, and as we held our sides, I wondered what this cuckoo summer would bring.

ACKNOWLEDGEMENTS

Much gratitude to Robert Kirby at United Agents who bottle fed this book when it was a mere lamb! Thanks to Emily Talbot who added valuable input and led *Cuckoo Summer* to market. Cheers to Eloise Wilson who skilfully 'skirted' the fleece. Last, but definitely not least, I'd like to thank Charlie Sheppard for her great insights and expertise in clipping the story and spinning it into the best possible yarn it could make.

Many thanks to the Royal Literary Fund who provide fodder beet over cold winters for me and many other authors.

WHEN THE SKY FALLS

PHIL EARLE

1941. War is raging. And one angry boy has been sent to the city, where bombers rule the skies. There, Joseph will live with Mrs F, a gruff woman with no fondness for children. Her only loves are the rundown zoo she owns and its mighty silverback gorilla, Adonis. As the weeks pass, bonds deepen and secrets are revealed, but if the bombers set Adonis rampaging free, will either of them be able to end the life of the one thing they truly love?

'A magnificent story . . .
It deserves every prize going'
Philip Pullman

'An extraordinary story with
historical and family truth at
its heart, that tells us as much
about the present as the past.
Deeply felt, movingly written,
a remarkable achievement'
Michael Morpurgo